James Ussher, John Gwynn, Dublin Trinity College Library

On a Syriac Ms.

belonging to the collection of Archbishop Ussher

James Ussher, John Gwynn, Dublin Trinity College Library

On a Syriac Ms.
belonging to the collection of Archbishop Ussher

ISBN/EAN: 9783337235826

Printed in Europe, USA, Canada, Australia, Japan

Cover: Foto ©Andreas Hilbeck / pixelio.de

More available books at **www.hansebooks.com**

[WITH TITLE-PAGE AND CONTENTS, VOLUME XXVII.]

THE

TRANSACTIONS

OF THE

ROYAL IRISH ACADEMY.

VOLUME XXVII.

———

POLITE LITERATURE AND ANTIQUITIES.

———

VIII.—*On a Syriac MS. belonging to the Collection of Archbishop Ussher.* By
VERY REV. JOHN GWYNN, D.D.

———

DUBLIN:
PUBLISHED BY THE ACADEMY,
AT THE ACADEMY HOUSE, 19, DAWSON-STREET.
SOLD ALSO BY
HODGES, FIGGIS, & CO., GRAFTON-STREET.
AND BY WILLIAMS & NORGATE,
LONDON: EDINBURGH:
14, Henrietta-street, Covent Garden.   20, South Frederick-street.

1886.

TRANSACTIONS : *Quarto, boards; or in Parts, stitched.*

Vols. I. to XXIII. (*some out of print*). For Prices, &c., inquire at the Academy.

Vol. XXIV.—Science (complete), 31s. 6d.

     ,,   Polite Literature (complete), 5s. } together (with Title), 24s.
     ,,   Antiquities (complete), 19s. 6d. }

Vol.   XXV.—Science (complete), 37s. 6d.   Vol. XXVI.—Science (complete), 35s.

ANSACTIONS, VOL. XXVII. (POLITE LITERATURE & ANTIQUITIES). Price to the Public.

Already Published.

	£	s.	d.
—On the Bell of St. Patrick, called the Clog an Edachta. By William Reeves, D.D.,	0	1	0
—On an Ogam Inscription. By Right Rev. Charles Graves, D.D., M.R.I.A., Lord Bishop of Limerick, &c. (With Plate I.),	0	1	0
—On the Croix Gammée, or Swastika. By Right Rev. Charles Graves, D.D., M.R.I.A., Lord Bishop of Limerick, &c. (With Illustrations),	0	1	0
—Fasciculus of Prints from Photographs of Casts of Ogham Inscriptions. By Sir Samuel Ferguson, LL.D. (With Plates I*. to V.),	0	2	0
—On Sepulchral Cellæ. By Sir Samuel Ferguson, LL.D.,	0	1	0
—On the Patrician Documents. By Sir Samuel Ferguson, LL.D.,	0	3	0
—On the Stowe Missal. By Rev. B. MacCarthy, D.D.,	0	6	0
—On a Syriac MS. belonging to the Collection of Archbishop Ussher. By Very Rev. John Gwynn. D.D. (With Title-page and Table of Contents to Volume),	0	2	0

VIII.—*On a Syriac MS. belonging to the Collection of Archbishop Ussher.*
By the Very Rev. JOHN GWYNN, D. D.

[Read, May 10, 1886.]

IT has long been a current statement in works on the criticism of the New
Testament, that Archbishop Ussher possessed a MS. unique in containing
the entire New Testament in Syriac. The existence of such a MS. has
been asserted, and its loss lamented, by several successive biblical scholars.
Bishop Marsh seems to have led the way, in the notes to his translation of
J. D. Michaelis's *Introduction* (1793). He cites (vol. II., p. 544) from the
London Polyglott (tom. v., p. 440) a note, in which Walton acknowledges
his obligation to Ussher's "*instructissima bibliotheca*" for the Syriac text of
the passage known as the *Pericope de Adultera* (John vii. 53—viii. 11); but
adds the remark—"Since that time [1657] no one has ever heard of this
MS. of Archbishop Ussher, nor is it enumerated in the catalogue of Ussher's
MSS. in the *Catalogus MSS. Angl. & Hib.*" In quite recent times, Dr. Tregelles, both in his *Introduction* (1860), and in Smith's *Dictionary of the Bible*
(1863, vol. III., Art. VERSIONS, ANCIENT SYRIAC), has pointed out that De Dieu
of Leyden, twenty-six years before Walton, had printed the same passage of
St. John, and had referred likewise to Ussher's MS. as its source. "It
appears (he says, *Introd.*, p. 282) from De Dieu that Archbishop Ussher
sent him a Syriac MS. containing *all* that is deficient in the Peshitto."
And again (p. 284): "If the MS. which De Dieu received from Ussher
could be traced and discovered, it would be of considerable value in relation to the question of the authorship of the supplementary parts of the
Syriac Version, as it seems to be the *only* copy of which we have any

knowledge which contains *every part* of the N. T. in Syriac." And so lately
as 1883, Dr. Scrivener has written to the like effect in the last edition of
his invaluable *Introduction to the Criticism of the N. T.* (p. 315).

I propose, accordingly, to trace the MS. in question; and to show that it
is not lost, but is and has been for more than 200 years in the possession
of Trinity College, Dublin; and farther, that its contents have been misdescribed in such a manner as to have hitherto prevented its identification,
and caused it to be overlooked.

The MS. which I thus identify as that which De Dieu and Walton have
referred to, is catalogued as B. 5. 16. Its bulk is inconsiderable, and it can
claim no venerable antiquity. It is a small quarto, written on paper; its
age is little more than two centuries and a-half; and its present binding
(dating, I am told, about 1820) gives it quite a modern appearance. But I
hope to show that its history and contents are sufficiently interesting to
warrant me in inviting attention to the account of it which I now proceed
to give.

It is written entirely in the Syriac language, in the cursive character
usually found in Syriac printed books and in MSS. of recent date, often called
Maronite. It consists of two distinct divisions, of which the *first* is exclu-
sively biblical, containing not by any means the whole N. T., but only the
following portions of it:—(1) The *Pericope de Adultera;* (2) the Four Minor
Catholic Epistles (2 Peter, 2 & 3 John, and Jude); (3) the Apocalypse.
The *second* division contains a tractate of Ephraim Syrus, 'On the Love of
Wisdom and Knowledge.' It is with the *first* of these two divisions that I
am about to occupy the space at my disposal: a few words will convey all
that I have at present to say about the *second*.

The principle of association on which the six portions of Scripture
which I have mentioned are here brought together, is evident on the face
of it. They are, as is well known, the portions of the N. T. which are not
contained in the ancient Peshitto, the Syriac Vulgate.

When the Syriac N. T. was sent to Europe by Ignatius, Jacobite Patriarch of Antioch, about the middle of the sixteenth century (1552), and
first printed at Vienna (1555) under the auspices of the Emperor Ferdinand,
these deficiencies were at once noticed. Widmanstadt, the editor, apologizes

for them in two notes, prefixed to the Gospels and to the Catholic Epistles
severally; and in the subjoined Epistle to Georgius Gienger and Jacobus
Jonas he affirms that the portions in question are extant in Syriac, and
that Moses of Marden, the agent whom Ignatius had commissioned to
procure the printing of the Syriac text, had gone back to his native Mesopotamia, and would bring copies of them with him on his return thence.
It is now admitted on all hands that the Peshitto (from whatever cause)
never included these parts of the N. T. as it is usually received in the
West. But it seems that Widmanstadt, and the scholars of the sixteenth
and even of the following century, attributed the absence of them from his
edition to the defectiveness of the Patriarch's MS. Accordingly we find
that our own illustrious Ussher, when he began to collect MSS. of Oriental
versions of the Scriptures, before the first quarter of the seventeenth century
was completed, had instructed an agent in the East to procure for him a
Syriac version of the missing portions of the N. T. None of Ussher's
letters to this person (Thomas Davies, a British merchant at Aleppo) is
preserved; but the purport of the instructions given may be gathered from
Davies' replies, six of which are printed in Parr's *Life of Ussher*, and re-
printed in Elrington's (Letters 71, 73, 90, 102, 116, 125), together with two
which had escaped Parr (388 and 401). The first of this series, dated
August 29, 1624, acknowledges one from Ussher, which apparently con-
veyed his first directions concerning the purchase of Syriac and other MSS.
Davies' subsequent letters relate his successes and failures, the difficulties
and delays that hindered the execution of his commission: and so early as
January 162$\frac{3}{3}$, he writes as follows:—"Those parcels of the N. T., viz.,
the History of the Adulterous Woman, the second Epistle of St. Peter, the
second and third of John, the Epistle of Jude, with the book of the Revelation, I have procured, and sent them, together with the five books of Moses,
and a small tract of Ephraim, by the ship *Patience* of London" (Letter 102).
In this passage (it is to be observed) the mention of "the five books of
Moses" is to be read parenthetically, for they have been described just
before as a distinct purchase. In another letter (90), which, though it
stands before the one I have quoted, I shall presently show (p. 281) by
internal evidence to be misplaced, and to belong to the latter half of 1626,

Davies inquires whether "the five books of Moses, with those parcels of the
N. T. (which your Lordship writ for) in the Chaldean tongue, sent you ten
months ago," had come safely to hand ?　In the former letter he had
explained that he uses the words "Chaldean" and "Syrian" as synonymous.
I may remark, in passing, that in those days letters from Aleppo were
often six, and apparently never less than four, months in reaching Ireland.
In this case the books sent in January seem to have been received in June,
1626, by Ussher, who was then in London.　He writes thence on the 23rd of
that month to Dr. Ward at Oxford (Letter 110), to inform him that he had
"received out of Mesopotamia an old MS. of the Syrian translation of the
Pentateuch"; and also had "received" (but he does not state from what
source) "the parcels of the N. T. which hitherto we have wanted in that language (viz., the History of the Adulterous Woman, the 2nd Epistle of Peter,
the 2nd and 3rd Epistles of St. John, the Epistle of Jude, and the Revelation); as also a small tractate of Ephraim Syrus in his own language."
Here it is to be observed that the tractate of Ephraim is again associated
with the "parcels of the N. T."　References to this MS. recur in his correspondence; but one only need be cited: it is in a letter (154) to De Dieu of
Leyden, dated October 1, 1629.　This eminent scholar had forestalled him,
as regards one important part of his acquisition, by publishing, in 1627, the
Revelation in Syriac from a MS. in the University Library of Leyden.
Ussher accordingly, in the letter referred to, compliments him on his publication, and informs him that he had diligently compared it with his own
MS.　Just about the time when Ussher was writing thus to De Dieu, another
noted Orientalist, Edward Pococke, who had found in the Bodleian Library
a MS. of the Syriac text of the Four Epistles I have mentioned, was com-
pleting at Oxford his edition of them, which he soon after entrusted to
De Dieu, under whose superintendence it was published at Leyden in 1630.
Thus the MS. sent by Davies to Ussher was not collated in time to serve as
basis for the text of these Epistles or of the Apocalypse; and the only new
biblical matter that remained for it to supply was the Syriac of the *Pericope
de Adultera.*　Accordingly, it appears that Ussher, shortly after the date of
this letter, with a liberality that was characteristic of his generous nature,
sent the MS. to De Dieu, who from it printed, in 1631, the *Pericope* in ques-

tion in his *Animadverss. in Quatuor Evangelia* (p. 443). De Dieu, in his note (*in loc.*) states (as mentioned above, p. 1) that he derives the passage from a MS. in Ussher's collection. He also describes the MS. as containing with it the Four Epistles and the Apocalypse; and in his Introduction more fully, as "exemplar MS. elegantissimo charactere Syro exaratum, *addito etiam beati Ephrem tractatu De Amore Sapientiæ.*" Not long after, in 1634, De Dieu published his *Animadvv. in Acta Apostolorum*, and in his dedication of it to Ussher renewed his acknowledgments for the favours he had received from him; the first being that he had presented him with a Samaritan Penta-teuch (this was in 1629, at the time of the letter I have cited, 154); and the second, that he had, two years after (that is, in 1631), sent him a MS. con-taining "*omnia N. T. Syriaci quæ in prioribus deerant editionibus, et præterea prolixum Ephræmi De Amore Sapientiæ tractatum.*" Further benefactions are then mentioned, of which I shall have occasion to say something presently.

I have thus traced the history of the MS. sent by Davies in January 1626, until it reached De Dieu's hands, and was used by him, in 1631. That the MS. whence Walton derived the Syriac text of John vii. 53–viii. 11 for his Polyglott was the same, is certain; and since Tregelles first pointed it out no one has questioned it. Thus it appears distinctly that I have established one of the points which at the outset I undertook to prove—that the MS. referred to by Walton and De Dieu as the authority for this passage has been misdescribed. The statements I have collected—from Davies, who procured the MS., from Ussher its owner, and from De Dieu, who edited the only part of it that has been published—all concur in assuring us that it contained not the whole Syriac N. T., but only the six portions of it which were wanting from the Peshitto. But it is as a complete and conti-nuous Syriac N. T. that it has been described by the modern writers who have supposed it to be missing, and desired its recovery. "De Dieu assures us (writes Dr. Scrivener, 3rd ed., p. 316) that the Ussher MS. contained *the whole* N. T., which no second copy of the Peshitto or any other Syriac version yet known has been found to do." Tregelles' description of it to the same effect, both in his *Introduction* and in the *Dictionary*, I have already referred to. In both places he gives as his authority the words of De Dieu's dedication which I have cited, "*omnia N. T. Syriaci quæ deerant.*"

But in the latter work he betrays a misgiving as to the accuracy of this construction of De Dieu's words, by adding in a note the query, "Does this mean that it merely contained what was wanting previously, or the *whole* including such parts?" And he proceeds to adduce (but unfortunately from Todd's *Life of Walton*, vol. i., p. 194, not from either of the *Lives* of Ussher, where he would have found the solution of his doubt) Ussher's own description of his MS., in the letter (110) I have already cited, "I have received the parcels of the N. T. which hitherto we have wanted in that [Syriac] language." Here the word "parcels" obviously indicates a collection of separate portions, not a continuous whole : but Tregelles prefers to abide by his misinterpretation of the sentence, and to wrest it into meaning an entire N. T.,* on the ground that "it seems strange if this section of St. John stood alone." It will presently appear how much misapprehension is involved in these words : for the present it suffices to point out that they are refuted by the first page of the MS. actually before us, in which that section does "stand alone."

I assume then, as the result of the evidence adduced, that the MS.

---

* I may here state that no MS. of the whole N. T. in Syriac is now known to exist. The famous copy in the Cambridge University Library (Oo. i. 1, 2) gives the Peshitto complete, with the Four Minor Epistles subjoined in the ante-Harklensian version, but lacks the Apocalypse ; as does also the recent important acquisition of the same Library (Add. 1700), which gives all the other N. T. books in the Harklensian version, and adds the First and (so-called) Second Epistle of Clement of Rome to the Catholic Epistles. The MS. No. 184 in the Library of the Seminary of Remonstrants, Amsterdam, of A. D. 1470, seems to have originally contained the N. T. *minus* the Apocalypse : but to the Four Epistles (which like Oo, i, 1, 2, it gives in the older version) it appends two attributed to the same Clement, *On Virginity*, which were published by Wetstein from this MS. in 1752. (See Bp. Lightfoot's *Clement of Rome*, pp. 15, 238 ; Beelen, *S. Clem. R. Epp. de Virginitate*, Prolegg., pp. x, xiii, xvii ; and Wetstein, *Duæ Epp. S. Clem. R.*, Prolegg.). For this MS. see farther, note below, p. 318. Ridley's two MSS. (New Coll. Oxon. 333, 334) are described below, pp. 289, 304. I find only one record of the existence of a complete MS. Syriac N. T., as follows :—"Novum Testamentum Syriace, cum versione Latina, Andreæ de Leon Zamorensis, juxta ipsius verba in Ep. ad Mich. Le Jay, p. 189. *Antiquit. Eccl. Orient.* 'Novi Testamenti textum Syriacum Paulo V. tradidi correctum, Latine quoque redditum, cum Apocalypsi tribus [?] que Epistolis, et Historia Adulteræ, quæ desiderantur in Bibliis Regiis : Pontifex vero commisit hæc omnia Card. Bellarmino' " (Le Long, *Biblioth. Sacra* [Bœrner's ed., 1709], tom. i., p. 184).

sought for is one not of the whole Syriac N. T., but only of the six portions specified, viz., the section John vii. 53–viii. 11, the four minor Catholic Epistles, and the Apocalypse. And without going farther, I might already fairly claim to have made out a strong case for identifying the Trinity College MS. before us as the missing MS. It contains exactly these six portions of the N. T., and no others. No second MS. answering the description is known to exist, or has ever been recorded as existing, in any British Library; nor I believe in any Library elsewhere—* certainly not in that of the University of Leyden. No writer on the Syriac N. T. has described any such MS. It was unique, so far as our information extends, as regards the combination of its contents, among the MSS. brought from the East up to and in Ussher's time: as in our own time the Trinity College MS. is in like manner unique among Syriac MSS. known to scholars. And if the combination of these six portions were arbitrary as well as unique, I might regard the identification as sufficiently proved, and close here. But the combination, as I have pointed out, so far from being arbitrary, rests on a very obvious ground of association. It must be admitted as not improbable that some other seventeenth-century scholar as well as Ussher may have sought and obtained a copy of the portions of the Syriac N. T. not given in the then printed editions. And it may be suggested that Ussher's MS. may have been lost in the many removals of his library between the years 1641, when it was in the siege of Drogheda, and 1661, in which year it became the property of Trinity College :† or, as Tregelles supposed, it may have been retained by De Dieu, and may now be lying hid somewhere in Holland. And the MS. before us may have been acquired by the College otherwise; *e.g.*, as one of the gifts of Provost Huntingdon in the latter years of the century (1683–92), who was a great Orientalist, and might have procured the MS. while he was British Chaplain at Aleppo, 1671–1682. But there are many considerations to be taken into account against such hypotheses. It is unreasonable to imagine a possible MS. acquired by some

* The nearest approach to it that I can find is the MS. noted xxxi. in the *Catalogus Biblioth. Reg.* (Paris, 1739). But though its contents otherwise agree with the description, the Apocalypse is not among them.

† *Journal of the Irish House of Commons*, May 31, 1661.

other collector and given to the College, when it is certain that a MS. exactly corresponding with that which the College actually possesses was in Ussher's collection. The list of Ussher's MSS. as made over to the College is not in existence, so far as I know; but the alphabetical Catalogue of MSS. written in 1688 mentions this MS. (as noted A. 4), and states its contents accurately. This is the earliest dated evidence of its existence in the Library; but a local Catalogue,* apparently older, mentions it likewise. Neither of these Catalogues marks it as Ussher's, nor does the MS. itself contain his signature or any notes identifiable as written by him. But *prima facie* the presumption is, that any MS. not expressly noted as having come into the College Library from some other quarter came from Ussher. And it is noteworthy that these earliest Catalogues associate with it (then A. 4), as standing on the same shelf A, three other MSS. (A. 5, A. 6, and A. 11), two of them immediately beside it—all of which are still in the Library: all exactly similar to it in form, size, paper, and every other respect; all written, as the very marked handwriting shows, by the same Syrian scribe; and all bearing the inscription "*Jacobi Armachani*" in the great Primate's autograph. I may here mention that it is recorded twice over as A. 4 in the printed list of Usserian MSS. in Trinity College, Dublin, in the *Catalogus MSS. Angliæ & Hiberniæ* (1697), but in such wise that Marsh deserves no blame for failing (see p. 269) to find it—first under *Ephraim*, then under *Historia* [Adulteræ]! Again, the Trinity College MS. is dated; and its date, November, 1625, as given in the colophon at the end of St. Jude, suits Ussher's MS. well, if we suppose it to have been, as it probably was, a transcript made to Davies' order, and newly completed when he sent it in January, 1626. But into the question of these dates I shall have to go more fully just now. The facts I have brought together so far, form a body of evidence whose cumulative force I believe it would be hard to resist, even if the six "parcels of the N. T." (as Davies and Ussher call them) were all we had to go on in claiming for the MS. before us that it is the identical copy procured by Davies for Ussher, and sent by Ussher to De Dieu. But farther: with those N. T. "parcels" there was forwarded by

---

* These Catalogues are D. 1. 6 and D. 1. 7 in the Catalogue of MSS., T. C. D. See also D. 1. 8.

Davies, as he twice states, a Tractate of Ephraim; which statement Ussher confirms. Whether it was separate or not when so forwarded does not appear; but it is certain that when the N. T. "parcels" reached De Dieu it was bound with them so as to form one book. His words as I have cited them make this plain; and also inform us that the tract was entitled "*On the Love of Wisdom.*" Now the MS. before us contains, and the Catalogues prove that at least as early as 1688 it contained, with the biblical matter already specified, a Tractate of the same author, bearing the same title, of which no other copy is anywhere recorded. In view of this fact the proof becomes irresistible. That after the arrival of Ussher's MS. in 1626 a second Syriac MS. should have been imported into Ireland before 1688, containing exactly the same six portions of Scripture, is, as I have admitted (however improbable), a tenable supposition, because a definite reason is assignable why those six portions should be associated. But that two MSS. so imported should agree in subjoining to those six portions the same tract of Ephraim—a tract which as it stands in the T. C. D. copy is unique, and moreover bears no imaginable relation to the biblical matter which precedes—is incredible. I conclude therefore with confidence that this T. C. D. MS., B. 5. 16, is no other than the MS. procured by Davies, possessed by Ussher, and used by De Dieu.

Further proof may well seem superfluous; yet it may be worth while to test this conclusion by comparing the text of the *Pericope de Adultera* as contained in this MS. with that printed by De Dieu from the MS. sent by Ussher. I find the two texts to agree *verbatim et literatim*—a fact of weight, for every other existing copy of this passage in Syriac varies more or less from the printed text, and they all vary *inter se*. This agreement extends even to the heading of the section, which is in the MS. as in De Dieu's text and Walton's, "The Lesson which is concerning the sinful woman, which is not in the Peshitto" (.ܦܫܝܛܬܐ ܗܕ ܐܝܕܐ ܚܛܝܬܐ ܐܢܬܬܐ ܕܥܠ ܩܪܝܢܐ); and also to the words supplied at the end of the passage to join it on to the next verse (John viii. 12), "*When therefore they were assembled together,* Jesus spake, saying, I am the light of the world, *et cætera*" (ܩܡ ܕܟܠܗ ܢܘܗܪܐ . ܩܬܐܡܪ ܡ ܝܫܘܥ ܐܢܘܢ ܐܡܪ ܡ ܐܬܟܢܫܘ ܕܟܕ ܘܫܪܟܐ:). Again, the

vowel signs and diacritic points agree almost as perfectly as the conso-
nants; and this is not a necessary agreement, for the writer of the MS., as
is usual with Syrian scribes, inserts the vowels not uniformly, as in Hebrew,
but at his discretion, only where they seemed needed to prevent mistake.
There are little more than thirty vowels in the passage as it stands in the
MS. The printed text inserts none which is not in the MS., and omits but
three of those which the MS. inserts. Nor is this all. The writer of the MS.
employs indifferently (according to the usual practice) the two equivalent
sets of vowel signs, the Syriac (combinations of points), and the Greek
(letters borrowed from the Greek alphabet). The printed text reproduces
these faithfully—Greek letter for Greek letter, Syrian point for Syrian
point. Now, inasmuch as the equivalence of these two forms of vocalization
is absolute, so that the employment of this or that sign for any given vowel
is in every case purely arbitrary, this coincidence of usage between the MS.
and the printed text, complete and without exception as I find it to be,
cannot be the result of chance, and would alone suffice to identify the MS.
as the basis of De Dieu's text. Yet again, one contracted word only
(ver. 7, ܕܐܠܝܢ?) appears in the MS.; the same word and no other is found
contracted on De Dieu's page. And finally, one clear mistake only is to be
laid to the scribe's charge—the omission of a word from verse 11. This
mistake is not indeed reproduced in the printed text, but it is sharply chal-
lenged by De Dieu, who corrects it by supplying between brackets the
much-needed negative [ܠܐ] in the closing sentence, "Go and sin *no* more."
These brackets are perpetuated in Walton's Polyglott, where they are a
standing witness to the claim of our MS. to be the source of Walton's text
as of De Dieu's before it. It is to be added that this MS. has the undesir-
able distinction (analogous to that possessed by the "wicked" Bible) of
being the only one to omit this negative, which is duly given by the other
Syriac copies of the passage. Were it otherwise, one might naturally conclude that the ground of the omission of this much-disputed narrative from
the Syriac N. T. was a well-founded objection to the precept, as our MS.
gives it, "*Go and sin more*"!

Such, then, are the results of the comparison of the written with the
printed text. The internal evidence thus obtained is at least as convincing

as the external evidence already adduced. It is not too much to say, that even if this MS. came before us without a particle of the ample external attestation I have produced, we should be obliged to admit its identity with that from which De Dieu derived his text, as proved to demonstration.

I know of but two difficulties that remain in the way of this conclusion, now that the difficulty arising from the misdescription of Ussher's MS. has been removed. One, as I have said, has been raised by Tregelles. De Dieu, in his profuse acknowledgments of Ussher's benefits, appears to speak of the MS. as *given* by Ussher to him: and Tregelles accordingly writes, " The MS. itself had been sent as *a present* to De Dieu " (*Introd.*, p. 284 ; *Dict.*, p. 1636). But a careful reading of De Dieu's words dispels this misconception. He first expresses his gratitude for the *gift* of a Samaritan Pentateuch, and then for other favours which he clearly distinguishes from it as being *loans.* As regards the former, he describes himself as being " amplissimo *munere beatus* "; as regards the MS. containing the six N. T. portions and the Tractate of Ephraim, and many other MSS. which he enumerates, he uses the verbs " *mittere,*" " *transmittere,*" merely. It is unlikely on the face of it that even Ussher, generous as he was, would give away a MS. which he so highly prized, and whose contents were so rare, in part unique. In point of fact, while his letters show unbounded liberality in lending* even

---

* E. g., to Selden several books (letter 98) ; to Const. L'Empéreur (a stranger to him) his MS. of the *Horreum Mysteriorum* of Gregory Barhebræus (192, 196) ; to Arnold Boate, his MS. of the *Catena in Evangg.* of Dionysius Barsalibæus (215). The last was duly returned, and is now in T. C. D. Library (B. 2. 9) : from it Dudley Loftus published in 1672 his *Exposition of Dionysius Syrus on St. Mark*, and in 1695 his similar volume on St. Matthew. It is evident that foreign scholars, even with no plea of personal acquaintance, freely applied to him for such loans in confident expectation of a favourable response. Much light is thrown by these letters, and others that follow them, on the generous character of Ussher, on his relations with contemporary men of learning in England and abroad, and on the arrangements for the interchange of letters and packets between England and foreign countries in his time. Thus, in 1632, we find him taking an opportunity of sending his Syriac Pentateuch to De Dieu by the hands of Frey, the travelling tutor of Viscount Dungarvan, eldest son of the Earl of Cork (then one of the Lords Justices of Ireland), who was at that time setting out from Dublin to make the "grand tour" (Letter 184 : see also 189). Other like instances occur in the correspondence. More regular means of transmission, through Dutch merchants and their London and Dublin correspondents, are indicated in Letter 154.

to strangers whatever treasures his library contained, I find no instance of his giving away any MSS. except those of which (as of the Samaritan Pentateuch) he possessed duplicates.* Moreover, I have traced some of the other MSS. which De Dieu mentions as " sent " or " transmitted " to him by Ussher, and I can prove that they were returned to their owner. Three are stated by De Dieu to have contained selections from Ephraim Syrus: these are mentioned by Ussher also (Letter 188) as sent by him to De Dieu; and one at least of them is identified, by his enumeration of its contents, with a MS. which I have already mentioned (p. 276) as being now in T. C. D. Library and bearing Ussher's autograph, formerly catalogued as A. 11 (now B. 5. 19). Another is the Syriac Pentateuch, already mentioned as sent by Davies along with our MS.; and a third is a Syriac Psalter. Both these Ussher reclaims as *loans*, writing to De Dieu in 1637 (Letter 210), " *remittas* Pentateuchum Syriacum et Psalterium quæ olim tibi *commodavimus*." His intention then was to use them in printing the Old Testament in Syriac; but this he never carried out. He must, however, have got them back, for he lent them not long afterwards to Walton, who used them for the Syriac O. T. text of his Polyglott. They are now in the Bodleian (the Pentateuch being Bod. Or. 121, and the Psalter, Bod. Or. 51).† Indeed De Dieu himself, in the very page where Tregelles supposes him to speak of the MS. in question as a gift, proceeds to express himself in terms which proved that he regarded it and the rest as *lent:* exclaiming, " omnia hæc MSS. . . . te in tam dissitas oras, per tot pericula, ad peregrinum hominem, *dubius an unquam esses recepturus, transmisisse !* " And there is no reason to doubt that he returned it and all the other MSS. to Ussher, as I have shown him to have done in the three cases which I have traced.

The other difficulty I have to notice arises out of the dates. I have said that the former division of our MS. is dated November 1625; I have to add

---

* Or triplicates: thus he gave Cotton a third copy of the Samaritan Pentateuch, retaining one which is now, I believe, in the Bodleian (Letter 148; see Macray's *Annals of the Bodleian*, p. 107; and cf. *Cat. MSS. Angl. and Hib.*, p. 156). Again, of his three copies of the Arabic Psalter he gave one to Laud; another, which he lent to Bedwell, seems to have been lost (Letter 184).

† Walton, *Polyglott*, tom. I., Prolegg., p. 80: Payne Smith, *Catal.*, pp. 28, 52.

that the latter division is dated 1626 (no month). Now Davies' letter (102) states that he sent the MS. on or before 16th January 1625. So far all is consistent; for Davies no doubt followed the then English style, and his date is to be understood as 26th January 1626 :* while the Syrian scribe (whom for the moment I assume to be a Maronite) would follow the Gregorian style (which was adopted in 1606 in the Maronito Church†), and reckon 1626 from 1st January. We have therefore only to suppose that the second division of the MS. was completed so early in January as to be ready to be placed in Davies' hands before the 26th.

But a doubt seems to be cast on this conclusion by a letter (90) which stands before this in Elrington's collection (as in Parr's), in which Davies inquires concerning the safe arrival of " the five books of Moses, with those parts of the N. T. which your Lordship writ for, . . . sent you *ten months ago*." This letter is dated July 1625, the day of the month not being specified. If this were correct, the MS. referred to must have been sent in the autumn of 1624, and therefore could not be ours, neither part of which was completed (see p. 276) before November 1625. But it is quite certain that this letter is misplaced, and that its date has been either misprinted or wrongly supplied by Parr's conjecture. For as it was written ten months after the sending of the MSS. specified, it must be nearly ten months later than the letter (102) written, as we have seen, in January 1626, which speaks of them as then just sent. And a comparison of the other contents of these two letters gives a like result. In Letter 102 Davies gives as " the news from Bagdat," which city was then in the hands of the Persians, that its siege by the Turkish Vizier was then in its third month. In Letter 90 he speaks of the siege as at an end, and relates how the Vizier had been forced to raise it at the end of eight months, and after several marches and disasters, had fallen back on Aleppo, and proposed to winter there.‡ I infer, therefore,

---

* The internal evidence of the letter proves that this is so: for it speaks of a letter, in answer to one of September 1624, as " received 8th of *July past*," which must mean July 1625.

† By the Patriarch, Joseph II. (Assemani, *Bibl. Or.* i., p. 558 ; quoting the *Chron.* of Steph. Edenensis).

‡ Cf. Rycault's *Hist. of the Turkish Empire* (1687), pp. 5, 6.

that this letter belongs to the autumn (probably October) of 1626. It is perhaps the letter " of the 20th October, per the ship *Rainbow*," mentioned in Davies' letter (388) of 13th March 162$. It is certainly prior, but not much prior, to Letter 116, written by Davies on the 14th November 1626 in reply to one in which Ussher, writing 31st July 1626, acknowledged the receipt of "the books sent by the ship *Patience*."

Thus the comparison of these letters, which at first sight seemed to cast a doubt on our MS., proves on examination to confirm the note of identity yielded by the dates. All the facts of the case fit in, when we assume that Ussher's MS. was a transcript made to Davies' order, in 1625 and the early days of 1626, and delivered to him by the scribe in time to be forwarded on the 26th of January of that year. The question is thus raised : Where was the MS. written ? and the probability suggests itself that it was somewhere not very far from Aleppo. Now, three or four quarters are indicated in Davies' letters whence he hoped to procure MSS. : Jerusalem and Damascus, (but these, as it seems, for Samaritan MSS. only); Amid (Diarbckr) in Mesopotamia; and the Lebanon country. Amid seems too remote to be a probable source for our MS.,* and there remains therefore the Lebanon. This is the obvious quarter to look to for its origin, for the style of the writing seems to be Maronite. Besides, Davies' letters (see 71, 102, 90, 116, 388, 125) show that from 1624 he was for two or three years in active negotiation for MSS. with the Maronites of that region ; and that there he procured the only other new transcript of any part of Scripture which he is known to have sent to Ussher—a copy of the Old Testament in Syriac, wanting only the Psalms. This copy was completed (Letter 125) on Davies' order, and forwarded more than two years after our MS., in 1628 ; its subsequent history is the same as that of the Syriac Pentateuch and Psalter I have already mentioned, and it is now with them in the Bodleian, bearing date 1627, and catalogued as Bod. Or. 151.† These facts suggested to me the idea that a comparison with this Bodleian MS. might lead to a

---

* Ussher seems (Letter 127) to speak of it as coming from Amid ; but he is merely repeating the account given by Davies (102, 110), which really relates to the Pentateuch MS. only.

† Walton, *ut supra* (p. 280); Payne Smith, *Cat.* p. 280.

more definite conclusion with respect to the origin of ours. Accordingly I have taken the T. C. D. MS. to Oxford, and have placed the two side by side. The result is, as I anticipated, that ours proves to be written in the unmistakable hand of the scribe who wrote the earlier and greater part of the Bodleian O. T. In a colophon appended to the Book of Susanna he gives us all particulars of persons, place, and time, as follows, f. 3346 : " Here ends this book by the help of our Lord Jesus Christ, in the year of Christ, 1627, in the month Thammuz [July], on the first day at the sixth hour, by the hands of a man sinful and vile, dust of the highways and dirt of the dunghill, the miserable Joseph, son of David, of the city beloved and blessed of Christ, Van of Mount Lebanon. It was written in the Monastery of Kenobin in the days of our venerable and blessed father Mar Peter, whose name is Mar John, Antiochian Patriarch. . . . ." This Joseph, then, was the scribe of both these MSS., and also of the other three in T. C. D. Library, which I have referred to (p. 276) as being in the same hand (B. 5.17, 18, 19 ; formerly A. 5, 6, 11). He is probably the person* whom Davies (Letter 90, cp. 116) " sent to Libanus to take a copy " of the " only one old copy of the O. T. extant" among the Syrians of those parts, which was " in the custody of the Patriarch of the Maronites, who hath his residence in Mount Libanus, which he may not part with on any terms; only there is liberty given to take copies thereof, which of a long time hath been promised me." In making this transcript of the O. T. he was assisted, as two entries in the MS. show (ff. 569 b, 600 b), by one Cyriacus, " Jacobite priest and monk," whose very different hand shows itself in a large part of the latter portion of it. The prelate named in Joseph's subscription is known as John XI. [Macluphius],† Maronite Patriarch 1609–1633 ; his other name, Peter, being that borne officially by all Patriarchs of this Church,‡ as that of

---

* The "minister of the sect of the Marranites, and by birth a Chaldean, but *no scholar*" (Letter 71), with whom Davies first tried to deal, seems to be a different person, and to have disappointed him (see 90).

† Le Quien, *Oriens Christ.*, tom. iii., col. 68.

‡ *Ib.*, 46, 65. The designation *Antiochenus* was given by the See of Rome to these Patriarchs, beginning (as it seems) from the time when Hieremias II. attended the Fourth Lateran Council (1215) ; see Le Quien, *ib.* 6, 41, 50. Syriac writers trace the title back to the time of Joannes Maro, *circ.* 700 (Steph. Edenens. *ap.* Assem. *B. O.* i., pp. 496–503).

Ignatius by the Jacobite Patriarchs. The monastery of Kenobin (= Κοινόβιον) was founded by Theodosius in the fourth century; and has been the seat of these Patriarchs since the time of John X., who died there in 1445. It has been visited and described by many travellers, who are eloquent in their admiration of the sublime beauty of its rock-hewn site on the western slope of Lebanon. In its library, then, was the original MS. of the Syriac O. T. which the Patriarch was bound (no doubt by an anathema inscribed in it, such as is often found in Syriac MSS.) not to sell, though he permitted the copy now in the Bodleian to be made from it:—and with it, no doubt, the originals of those " parcels of the N. T. " which the T. C. D. MS. contains ; and probably the originals likewise of the Tractate of Ephraim, and other like matter, which are found in the other MSS. written by the same Joseph.* It may still retain these treasures, and others well worth looking after. Burckhardt indeed, writing in 1810, described it as being, when he visited it, empty of the books it once possessed : but Lord Lindsay (afterwards Earl of Crawford), twenty-seven years later, in 1837, saw several, both MSS. and printed, in the Church. He especially mentions one, a Syriac Bible (possibly the archetype of the Bodleian copy) kept apart in a chamber over the entrance gate, but so carelessly that, as he rode up, some leaves of it " flew out of the window and lighted at his feet."† Possibly it may not yet be too late for some explorer to rescue what remains of these treasures, if their present guardians should prove to be as open to negotiation as the monks of the Nitrian Monastery, whence so rich a

---

* Apparently it contained also a copy of part at least of the Syro-Hexaplar O. T. version of Paul of Tella ; for to this Bodleian O. T. are appended 1 [3] Esdras and Tobit, both headed "according to the LXX." Of these, the latter has been shown by Dr. Ceriani (*Le Versione Siriache*, p. 22) to belong (in part) to that version, by comparison with the citations of Tobit, given by Andr. Masius (*Syrorum Pecul.*) from his lost Syro-Hexaplar MS. I have in like manner identified this 1 [3] Esdras as Syro-Hexaplar by means of one of the Nitrian MSS. of the British Museum (Add. 12168), a Catena which among other extracts expressly described as from the version of Paul, gives the following portions of 1 [3] Esdras :—ii. 1-16, 24, 25 ; iv. 38-40, 49-57 ; v. 47-vi. 2 ; vii. 6-viii. 29 ; viii. 69-78 ; viii. 93-ix. 10 ; ix. 46, 47—all of which agree with the text as first printed by Walton from Uss., *i.e.*, Bod. Or. 151.

† *Letters*, pp. 852, ff. (edition of 1858).

store of Syrian MSS. has within these last fifty years been acquired for the British Museum.*

I have thus traced the journeyings of our MS. from Kenobin on Mount Lebanon, by way of Aleppo, to Ireland, and thence to Leyden and back. It must have resumed its place among Ussher's books before his death, and have been seized with the rest by Cromwell, and deposited in Dublin Castle; and thence have been transferred, as part of that splendid collection, by order of the Irish House of Commons, May 1661, in the name of King Charles II., to its present and rightful abode in Trinity College. But an incidental question arises here, which needs a word in reply. Did our MS. ever come into Walton's hands? I am confident it did not. He refers to it, as I have said, for the *Pericope de Adultera*, but nowhere else. There is no trace of his using it for the text of the Epistles or of the Apocalypse: in fact the Syriac *variæ lectiones* of his Polyglott (tom. VI., iii.), as collected for him from MSS. by Thorndike, relate to the O. T. only; while for the N. T. he was content to follow printed texts, chiefly that of the Paris Polyglott (*ib.* p. 50). The text of this *Pericope* (unless Ussher sent him a transcript of it from the MS.) he probably derived from De Dieu's, with which it agrees *literatim*, even to the heading prefixed, and the bracketted [ܗ]. No change is made except that the vowels are fully supplied, so as to correspond with the full vocalization adopted throughout Walton's N. T. text. Had the MS. before us been lent, as Ussher's other three MSS. which I have specified were lent, to Walton, it would not be now in Trinity College Library. Those three MSS., with others, after Ussher's death in 1656, remained with Walton. After Walton's death in 1661 they were treated as his (whether by right of purchase or by mistake); and when Walton's collection was sold in 1683,† they (three at least of them) were purchased

---

* As an example of the reluctance of Syrian ecclesiastics to let the contents of their libraries be known, see the reply of the Maronite Patriarch, Stephen II. (Edenensis) to Huntington, in which, only fifty years after Davies obtained these transcripts for Ussher, he disclaims all knowledge of MSS. existing at Kenobin or elsewhere (*Life*, p. viii, prefixed to Smith's edition of Huntington's *Epistolæ*, 1704).

† Todd's *Life of Walton*, I. 160.

by the University of Oxford.*   Thus it appears that Trinity College owes acknowledgments to De Dieu, not only directly, as the honest restorer of the MS. he borrowed, but also indirectly, as the means of keeping it from passing, as all the other MSS. of Ussher's collection which are cited in Walton's Polyglott have passed into the Bodleian.

I proceed now to give a detailed account of the composition of the MS., and of its contents:—

The sheets of paper (very thick, and smoothed so as to resemble parchment) of which it is made up are arranged in quires, mostly of five sheets, but occasionally of less.   Thus, as the book now stands, its first quire has but four sheets, and likewise its last; while the first, or biblical, division of it ends with a half-quire of two sheets.   The leaves bear no numbering, but the quires are numbered in the usual Syrian manner with Syriac letters, except two half-quires of inferior paper which have been inserted (apparently by the original Syrian binder) before and after the five quires which contain the Apocalypse.   These five quires are numbered 1 to 5; while the quires which stand before them (containing the *Pericope* and the Four Epistles) are marked 6 and 7.   It thus appears that the scribe originally arranged the seven quires which formed the *first* or biblical division of the MS., so that the Apocalypse should stand first, and that the *Pericope* with the Four Epistles should follow it.   We cannot tell whether he had any precedent for disposing them in this order; for, as to these Epistles, the few Syriac MSS. which exhibit them as part of the N. T. place them variously; and as to the Apocalypse, we have, as will presently appear, no manuscript evidence at all of its place in the Syriac canon.   But no doubt when he changed them into their present order he did so in order to adapt his work to the Western ideas of the purchaser.   The rest of the book, *i. e.*, the *second* division of it, containing Ephraim's Tractate, consists of four quires, which are numbered separately 1 to 4.   In both parts the headings of the books, and also the appended subscriptions, are written in vermilion.   In the punctuation also vermilion is used throughout: two red spots placed colonwise, with a black

* Macray's *Annals of the Bodleian,* pp. 107, 126, Cp. *Cat. MSS. Angl. and Hib.,* p. 156; Walton *Polygl.* I., pp. 77, 81; vi. iv. p. 1.

spot between, serving for a colon or period; while paragraphs are divided by the usual lozenge of four red spots surrounding a black mark, usually an irregularly circular ring. These lozenges are uniformly used throughout the text of Ephraim, and pretty regularly in the Apocalypse; but in the two preceding quires but two occur—one in the middle of 2 Peter, one at the end of Jude. In the *first* division the vowels also are mostly given in vermilion, but some also in black; the latter no doubt written with the letters, and the former supplied afterwards. These red vowels are very capriciously added or omitted; but on the whole they are most frequent in the early chapters of the Apocalypse, and rarer in later quires. In the *second* division they are not found at all; and the few vowels that are written are in black. The chief points, including *ribui*, are in black all through the MS. In the *first* division elaborate head-pieces in black and red are prefixed to the *Pericope* and to the Apocalypse, and a simpler one to 2 John: and a similar one stands at the beginning of the *second* division. The use of vermilion has proved unfortunate, for the pressure the book has undergone when last bound has transferred a good deal of the pigment from page to opposite page, in some places glueing the leaves together so as to injure the surfaces when they are separated. With this exception, the excellent handwriting of the scribe is as legible as when it first came from his pen. The other specimens of his handiwork in the T. C. D. collection are by no means so uniformly good; being in parts carelessly and roughly written with inferior ink on paper imperfectly smoothed. In one of them (B. 5, 19, formerly A. 11), which contains extracts from Ephraim, several leaves are written in another hand—I believe that of the Cyriacus who has signed the Bodleian O. T. MS. as his collaborator.* I am sorry to add that the disparaging epithets which, in the colophon cited at p. 283, " Joseph, son of David " so freely takes to himself, are proved by this MS. to be by no means unmerited. The MS. is made up as follows. First come nine short tractates of Ephraim, of which the ninth (ending a quire) is left incomplete, all in the writing of Joseph. Then follow two quires in the writing of his assistant, who had, as it appears, chanced to begin a copy of the same collection,

* I cannot affirm this positively, not having compared this MS. side by side with Bod. Or. 151.

for'these quires simply repeat the Tractates which stand first and second, but are inserted as if they were new matter. And that this is no oversight, but done with design of utilizing them to swell the book, is evident, for they are continued in the hand of Joseph, and numbered continuously with the preceding quires. He then begins a new Tractate (the 10th, or as he numbers them, the 12th), breaks off abruptly in the second page, and so closes the volume; which Davies, being, as he tells us, unable to read Syriac, or to find any adviser who could read it, bought and sent to Ussher, in ignorance of the fraud practised on him. Two *marginalia* in Ussher's hand note this repetition of the first and second Tractates. I may here mention that for this and other similar Ephraim MSS. in T. C. D., and the Bodleian transcript of the whole O. T., and a MS. Syriac Grammar (also in T. C. D.), together with sundry Samaritan fragments, Davies appears to have paid on Ussher's behalf but £39 18s. (Letter 401 ; cp. 388, 125). I find no state-ment of the cost of our MS.; the only one priced separately is the O. T. transcript, the original estimate for which was £10 (Letter 71).

But to return to our MS. The *Pericope de Adultera* begins on the recto of the first leaf (as the quires now stand), and ends on the recto of the second. I have already mentioned how it is headed, and how terminated; and that De Dieu reproduces it faithfully in both points. Walton, though (as I have said) he retains the heading, rejects the modification of viii. 12 * with which it closes, and reads that verse as in the Peshitto and Greek—"Again then Jesus spake unto them, saying, . . ." The end of the passage is marked in the MS. by the usual ܣܠܡ (= *explicit*), prolonged across the page.

Our MS., though the first authority from whence this passage was made known as existing in Syriac, is not now the only one. Three others have since come to light.† Of these copies, much the earliest (*a*) is in the British Museum, written in a ninth-century hand on a leaf prefixed to a Peshitto MS. of the Gospels of the fifth or sixth century (Add. 14470). It is introduced by the following note:—"Yet another chapter from the

---

* This reading of viii. 12 is countenanced by two old Latin MSS.; b, which gives " *rursus autem congregatis illis,*" and e, " *iterum autem cum convenissent.*"

† For two other MSS. said to contain the *Pericope,* see pp. 274, 275, notes.* I know nothing further of either.

Gospel of John son of Zebedee. This σύνταξις is not found in all copies; but the Abbat Mar Paul found it in one of the Alexandrian copies, and translated it from Greek into Syriac, according as it is here written; from the Gospel of John, canon tenth, number of sections 96,* according to the translation of Thomas the Harklensian." It then starts from vii. 50 ("Nicodemus saith unto them . . . ."), giving it and the two following verses as in the Harklensian text, then proceeds with the disputed passage, beginning vii. 53, and ends with viii. 12, modified as in our MS. A note nearly the same, but abridged, is found in a Paris MS. (XXII., *Catal. Bibl. Reg.*) of the Harklensian Gospels, dated A. Gr. 1503 (*i. e.*, A.D. 1192, not 1202, as Adler wrongly states), which also contains the *Pericope;* appended to, but not inserted in, St. John's Gospel. This copy (*b*) begins with vii. 53, and ends with viii. 11, to which it subjoins the note. Adler has printed the whole, *Verss. Syrr.*, p. 57. In the third copy (*c*) the *Pericope* takes its place in the text of the Gospel: this is another Harklensian MS., known as Cod. Barsalibæi, now in the Library of New College, Oxford (No. 334), from which White has printed the *Pericope* as an appendix to his edition of the Harklensian Gospels (p. 559). In this MS., viii. 12 is given in its altered form. A marginal note states that "this συντυχιον is not found in all copies"; when the Greek word, evidently a blunder for σύνταξις, points to a common origin with the notes in the two MSS. last mentioned. Thus in these three MSS. the *Pericope* appears associated more or less directly with the Harklensian version. But of the four extant copies of the *Pericope*, one only (*c*) is exhibited *in loco* as part of the Gospel; while the others stand apart from any context: a fact which if known to Tregelles would have saved him from misapprehending the nature of Ussher's MS. so widely as we have seen he did. The variations among the four copies are about a dozen, none being material. In one verse (viii. 5) all four differ: and in more than one reading each of them stands alone. The British Museum copy has not been printed, but I have transcribed it carefully, and find, as its superior age might lead one to anticipate, that its text is the best. The Paris copy,

* A mistake for 86. The number of sections in the Harklensian St. John is the same as in the Greek, 232 (Adler, p. 63; Rosen-Forshall, *Catal.*, p. 27; Wright, *Catal.*, p. 75; Payne Smith, *Catal.*, pp. 85, 89).

which is the only one of the four I have not seen, is not very correctly
printed by Adler, and seems, even after allowing for typographical errors,
to be the least accurately written.   The original of this version must have
differed considerably from all existing Greek copies; keeping at first pretty
close to the Textus Receptus, but approximating especially towards the end
to that of Cod. Bezæ (D), which is the oldest extant Greek of the passage.
It can hardly be doubted that the Abbat Mar Paul, who is stated to have
found the passage in Greek and made this translation of it, was Paul of
Tella, the translator of the LXX. into Syriac.   No other Syrian Paul is
recorded as a translator of Scripture, or as visiting Alexandria.   He is
known to have been there, engaged on his version of the O. T., in the same
year, 616, in which Thomas of Harkel was similarly at work on the New,
and actually under the same roof—of the Antonine monastery.[*]   Both were
Monophysite Bishops, seeking refuge there from troubles in Syria, together
with Athanasius, Monophysite Patriarch of Antioch.   The versions of both
are marked by the same servile manner of reproducing the Greek *verbatim*, at
whatever sacrifice of Syriac idiom.   Of this manner, the most conspicuous
feature is the expression of the possessive pronoun as a separate word by
means of the particle ܠܝ?, instead of suffixing it, after the Semitic use,
to the noun.   In the passage before us a possessive pronoun occurs, in
viii. 5, as read in three of the four copies, "Now in *our* law . . ." and they
render it accordingly, in this separate form, ܠܢ?.   In Ussher's MS. this
pronoun does not appear, perhaps correctly—certainly in conformity with
the best Greek text;[†] but at the cost of losing this mark of the translator's
hand.   If we assume, then, that the London and Paris MSS. rightly name
Paul as the translator of the *Pericope*—in other words, that the translation,
though not made by Thomas of Harkel, was made by a contemporaneous
and kindred hand—we have a fair explanation of the relation in which we
find it placed with regard to the Harklensian version, associated *with* it, yet

---

  [*] Cp. the Harklensian subscriptions (Adler, p. 45) with that of the Syro-Hexaplar MS.,
Add. 14437, in Wright's *Catal.*, p. 34) ; and see also Ceriani, *Monumenta Sacra et Prof.*, t. i.
fasc. i., *Prolegomena*, p. iii.

  [†] There is, however, good authority for ἡμῶν, and better for ἡμῖν.

not usually as *of* it. Another and an earlier translator had, however, been previously suggested. Dr. Gloucester Ridley, the original owner of the Cod. Barsalibæi, in his account of that MS. (*De Verss. Syrr. Indole*, p. 17), asserts that the passage in question was translated by Maras, Bishop of Amid,* also a Monophysite, in 522. Marsh, in his edition of Michaelis (pp. 545, 580), following Ridley incorrectly, attributes the translation to Mar Aba,† a very different person. Tregelles (*Introd.*, p. 282) corrects Marsh's blunder, but strangely makes another as to date; printing in his text 622, and from this false datum drawing the true conclusion that Maras cannot have been the translator: while in his note he cites the figures accurately as given by Ridley, DXXII. And further it is to be observed that both Marsh and Tregelles err in understanding Ridley to say that a note in Cod. Barsalib. is his authority for ascribing the translation to Maras in 522. That MS. contains no such note;‡ and Ridley in thus specifying the writer and date is but giving his own opinion. Before the evidence pointing to Paul of Tella came to light, this view of Ridley's was a very defensible one; having apparent support from Assemani, who (*Bibl. Or.*, II., pp. 53, 61) in his summary of the *History* of Zacharias Rhetor,§ mentions a version of this passage cited by Zacharias from this Maras. But the *History* of Zacharias is now accessible, having been published by Land (*Anecdota Syr.*, III.) from an early MS. (*circ.* 600) now in the British Museum (Add. 17202, see f. 144*b*); and the version of the *Pericope* it exhibits (bk. VIII. 7) proves to be not only distinct from that before us, but to give a redaction of the narrative differing widely from any other known form of it, Greek or translated. It is, moreover, cited with the sectional number 89 (instead of 86), which places it not before John viii. 12, but after John viii. 20.‖ And, moreover,

* Consecrated 519–20; banished soon after; lived at Alexandria from 527 till his death, 540.

† A Nestorian; Catholicus, 537; died 552.

‡ I have myself inspected the MS.; and Mr. Margoliouth, Fellow of New College, who has kindly examined it further, confirms what I have above stated.

§ Bishop of Mitylene, 536.

‖ I have compared the text of this passage in Add. 17202 with another copy in Add. 17193, and with that given by Dionys. Barsalib., in his *Commentary on the Gospels*, as exhibited by the Abbé Martin (*Introd.*, *Partie Prat.*, IV. p. 231) from two MSS., one being Add. 7184 of British

it appears that the work of Maras which contained this passage was written in Greek, and that the Syriac is due to the Syrian translator and continuator of Zacharias(see Land, *ut supr.*, Introd.). There is thus no ground for regarding Maras as a translator at all, and the claim of Paul to be accepted as the translator of the *Pericope* stands unaffected by the existence of this other earlier Syriac form of the same passage.* A version of the *Pericope* distinct from both the above is contained in the Jerusalem Syriac Lectionary. It also is printed by Adler (p. 190), and seems to approach nearer than that of Ussher's MS. to the text of Cod. Bezæ.

Museum. They agree substantially; though with some variations which make the sense here and there somewhat uncertain. I append a translation :—

"And it came to pass on a certain day, as Jesus was teaching, they brought unto him a certain woman which was found with child of adultery, and informed him concerning her. And Jesus said unto them (for he knew, as God, their lusts of uncleanness and their doings), In the law what does it command ? Then said they unto him, In the mouth of two or three witnesses she shall be stoned. But he answered and said unto them, According to the law indeed, one pure and free from these lusts of sin, and confidently and with authority (as being himself not guilty in this sin) bearing witness, let him bear witness against her and first cast a stone at her, and the next *likewise*, and let her be stoned. They then, because they were vile and guilty in this lust of transgression, went out one by one from before him and left the woman. And when they had gone forth, Jesus was gazing on the ground. And as he wrote on the dust thereof, he said unto her, Woman, these which brought thee hither, and were desirous to bear witness against thee, when they gave heed unto the things which I said unto them, which thou hast heard, have left thee and departed : Go thou also now, and do not this sin any more."

Zacharias prefaces the passage with this statement, that it belongs to John's Gospel, but is found in no other copy except that of Maras. All the above MSS. agree in referring it to "Canon (= section) 89." The relation pointed out by Ewald (*Die Johannischen Schriften*, p. 271 ; see Bp. Lightfoot in *Contemp. Rev.*, vol. xxvi., p. 847) between this narrative and John viii. 15 is well brought out by thus subjoining it to verse 20. The reference to a *second* witness in the version of Maras makes a further point of contact with verse 17. It is worth mentioning that the *Synopsis*, wrongly attributed to Athanasius, which however is a careful if not very ancient compilation, places (ch. 50) the *Pericope* immediately before verse 21.

* It is remarkable that this is the recension of the story cited by Dionys. Barsalib. in his *Commentary* (see last p., note ‖, also Assem. ii., p. 53) ; though in the Cod. Barsalibæi, which purports to be corrected by him (Ridley, p. 50), the other recension is given. The latter is also the recension known to Gregory Barhebræus (Assem. ii. 169).

Immediately after the final ܘܠܡ subjoined to the *Pericope*, on the recto
of the second leaf of our MS., stands the heading of the first of the Four
Minor Epistles, "Further we begin to write the Second Epistle of Peter
(ܟܬܒܝܢܢ ܬܘܒ ܐܓܪܬܐ ܕܬܪܬܝܢ ܕܫܡܥܘܢ ܟܐܦܐ). It ends f. 8 v°, and is sub-
scribed "Ends the Epistle of Peter the Apostle." Then comes a horizontal
rope ornament, in red and black, across the page; and then the heading,
"Second Epistle of John." The conclusion of this Epistle (f. 10 r°), and
the beginning of the Third, are similarly denoted, "Ends the Second
Epistle of John," and (without any break between) "Farther we write the
Third Epistle of John." At foot of f. 11 r° this Epistle closes with "Ends
the Third Epistle of John"; and at head of f. 11 v° we have "The Epistle
of Jude brother of James." The final colophon is subjoined to Jude,
f. 14 v°, being sixth of second quire, as follows: "Ends the Epistle of Jude
the Apostle (his prayer [be] with us. Amen). And the completion of it was
in Teshrin the latter [November], year 1625 of Christ" (ܫܠܡܬ ܐܓܪܬܐ ܕܝܗܘܕܐ
ܫܠܝܚܐ ܨܠܘܬܗ ܥܡܢ ܐܡܝܢ ܘܗܘܐ ܫܘܡܠܝܗ ܒܬܫܪܝܢ ܐܚܪܝܐ ܫܢܬ ܐܠܦ ܘܫܬܡܐܐ
ܘܥܣܪܝܢ ܘܚܡܫ). The remaining four leaves of the quire are left blank.

The text of these Epistles is the least valuable part of our MS. It does
not vary materially from Pococke's. Notwithstanding some errors, chiefly
of omission, it is rather more accurate than the latter, but its points of
superiority are mostly corrections of obvious mistakes which Pococke had
set right conjecturally in his notes. Pococke's MS. is still in the Bodleian
(Bod. Or. 119). When he printed his text from it in 1630 he was aware
(see his *Præf.*, and also De Dieu's *Præf.*, to Apocal.) that another copy had
previously been in the hands of Etzel,* a learned Jesuit of Mayence, whose
Latin version of these Epistles from this Syriac text is given by Nicolas
Serarius, also a Jesuit of Mayence, in his *Commentt. in Epp. Canon.* (Mayence,
1612), pp. 53, 54. In his *Prolegomena Biblica* (p. 80, quæst. 1) Serarius
states that this was a copy brought to Rome by Maronites, and that it contained the Apocalypse also. I find no record of it as now existing, nor can
I learn whether Moses of Mardon ever fulfilled his promise of bringing a
copy of these portions with him on his second visit to Europe, as De Dieu

* See Possevin, *Apparatus.*, s. v. *Balthasar Etzel.*

(*Præf.*, as above) affirms he did. But it seems to me certain, judging by the amount of deviation from Pococke's text shown by that printed soon after (in 1633) in the Paris Polyglott (which Walton adopted without change), that Gabriel Sionita, the editor of the Paris Syriac text, did not merely reprint Pococke's, with conjectural emendations, as is usually stated, but based his text on an independent MS.* A comparison of the Paris text of its Latin version with the Latin of Etzel satisfies me that Sionita's MS. must have been also distinct from that used by Etzel. If this be so, Sionita's MS. may probably be in some French Library. Possibly it may be identical with the MS. which, as I have stated above (p. 274, n.*), is mentioned by Le Long, in connexion with the name of Le Jay the publisher of the Paris Polyglott, as having been sent to Bellarmine, and which is described as containing the whole N. T. in Syriac, including all the supplementary portions. However this may be, it appears that more than one of the Syriac MSS. in the Bibliothèque Nationale in Paris contain these Epistles: and not a few † copies of them exist elsewhere. Of these, the most numerous and important belong to the Nitrian collection in the British Museum. Another, a valuable one, has recently been made known by Professor Isaac H. Hall, of Philadelphia; it is contained in the "Williams MS.," a copy of the N. T. wanting the Apocalypse; apparently of the fourteenth century. He has issued a beautiful photographic reproduction of the leaves which exhibit these Epistles, and their text is much better than that of Pococke's MS. I have collated with Pococke's text this of Ussher's, that of Williams', and three complete and two defective Nitrian copies; and have obtained from them ample materials for substantially amending the ordinary printed text.

* In this opinion I am confirmed by the judgment of Dr. Davidson. See his *Bibl. Criticism, N. T.*, p. 620 (edition 1854).

† Professor Hall (*Syrian Antilegomena*) says "six or seven," but this is an under-estimate. In British libraries alone there are not less than nine: in London six or more, Oxford one, Cambridge one, Dublin one. Professor Hall (in a paper quoted below) speaks of one MS. as being only a transcript from the Paris Polyglott. This seems very improbable. I do not know what MS. he refers to, but I venture to guess that it will prove to be the copy used by Gabriel Sionita; the original of the Paris text, not a copy from it. For the Amsterdam MS., formerly Wetstein's, see note * p. 274. Judging by the few specimens of its text given by Wetstein, it must be worth collating. (See farther, note at end, p. 313.)

One Nitrian MS. I would specially indicate, Add. 14623 : it is much the earliest existing authority for the Syriac text of these Epistles, bearing date A. Gr. 1134 (= A. D. 823) ; and shows, as might be expected, the purest text. A text critically revised on such authorities is a real desideratum ; not merely from the point of view of Syriac scholarship, but as an important contribution to the textual criticism of the Greek of this part of the New Testament. Dr. Scrivener (*Introd.* p. 646, n.[1]) justly characterizes this Syriac version as " well deserving careful study, . . . of great interest, and full of valuable readings." Where texts vary, it is found usually on the side of the oldest and best Greek MSS., and the instances in which it exhibits readings unsupported by good authority of MSS. or of versions, are not many. And I find that a text restored by means of the Nitrian and other early copies would approach still closer to the best Greek standard, and would be almost or altogether freed from the few anomalous or inferior readings which disfigure the text as printed. Professor Hall (*Journal of Soc. of Bibl. Lit. and Exegesis*, June–December, 1884, p. 42) has noted that one of these readings, ܟܠܘܣ ("in the *world*") for the similar ܟܠܘܣ ("in the *people*"), of 2 Peter ii. 1 is corrected in his MS. ; the Nitrian MSS. agree here with his against Pococke's (which latter Ussher's follows). Another, of more importance, is worth mentioning. It is well known that in 2 Peter iii. 10, for the usual reading (of A and L, and of most cursives) "the world and all the works therein shall be *burnt up*" (κατακαήσεται), most of the uncials, headed by ℵ and B, give " shall be *found*" (εὑρεθήσεται); *i. e.*, as the margin of our Revised Version renders, " shall be discovered." Hitherto this Syriac version has been cited by all critics as almost the sole authority (the Sahidic version seems to be the only other) for a reading unknown to Greek MSS., which, by inserting a negative before the verb, yields " shall *not be found*"; i. e., " shall be no more seen." And it is true that Pococke's MS. exhibits the "not" (ܠܐ), as does Ussher's and one Nitrian (Add. 17226). But the earliest Nitrian MS., which as I have said is 700 or 800 years older than these, agrees with the best Greek text, giving "*shall be found*," without the negative; and in this I find Professor Hall's MS. supports it. The margin of the Harklensian (which I am about to show preserves the readings of this version) also gives " shall be found"; (the [ܠ]

of White's edition is his interpolation). It is easy to understand how a scribe, taking on himself the function of critic, inserted the " not " to make sense out of an obscure expression which seemed to him unmeaning. Nay, I have lighted on direct evidence of the making of this interpolation. One of the Nitrian copies I have referred to (Add. 14473) is an eleventh-century appendix to a very early Peshitto MS., and is written in a clumsy imitation of the old estrangelo character—presumably therefore a transcript from an ancient estrangelo original. In this copy (which is second in age among the copies I have seen) the ل does not appear in the estrangelo text, but is inserted, I believe by the scribe himself, in the ordinary character in the margin. It is not often that one can thus catch a scribe (*flagrante delicto*) in the very act of tampering with the text of his exemplar. Here I venture to digress, so far as to mention another confirmation which I have just observed of this difficult reading. In the discourse usually known as the 2nd Epistle of Clement of Rome, which though admittedly not the work of that Father, is certainly a second-century composition, there is what seems a free citation from 2 Peter iii. 10, 12 (combined with Malachi iv. 1) in ch. xvi. (being one of the chapters recently recovered by Bryennios). It is as follows: τακήσονταί τινες τῶν οὐρανῶν, καὶ πᾶσα ἡ γῆ . . . ἐπὶ πυρὶ τηκόμενος, καὶ τότε φανήσεται τὰ . . . ἔργα τῶν ἀνθρώπων. This passage seems clearly to prove not only that 2 Peter was read in the second century, but read (as the last verb indicates) with εὑρεθήσεται in the verse in question. The correction of this reading is the most important one I have arrived at from the study of the copies I have referred to. But there are many others worth attending to. An analysis of my results for the first chapter of 2 Peter will give a fair idea of their amount. In this chapter I observe twenty-five places (most, but not all, of them noticed in Tischendorf's eighth edition of the Greek Testament) where Pococke's edition appears to yield evidence bearing on the Greek text. In eleven of these instances the Syriac seems to have no good authority on its side. But in four of them the translator has mistaken the meaning, or has been misunderstood. Of the seven that remain, five are corrected and disappear by collation of the copies I have used; and two real misreadings only are left—the omission of ἡμῖν (ver. 3), and the insertion of ὑμᾶς (ver. 8). In all these five corrections I have the authority of the oldest Nitrian MS.; in four of them it is supported by the second oldest in three by Professor Hall's; in but one by Usshor's. Taking this chapte then as an average example, it may be calculated that the text is likely to b improved by aid of these MSS. to the extent of the removal of five-seventh of the imperfections found in it as it stands in Pococke's edition.

The version being of so much value, it becomes matter of interest t inquire by whom and at what date it was made. Though we find ii Syriac writers no express reply to these questions, we have, I think, th means of answering them conclusively. Several scholars (Dr. Davidson, believe, most definitely; Professor Hall most recently) have conjectured tha in this version of these Epistles we have a surviving remnant of the trans lation of the N. T. which is recorded* to have been made A. D. 508 fo Philoxenus, Monophysite Bishop of Mabug, by his chorepiscopus Polycarp which is not otherwise extant except in a few minute fragments preserve(by Wiseman (*Hor. Syr.* p. 178). This suggestion may, as it seems to me be advanced out of the region of probable guesses, well-nigh into that o: demonstrated truths. The Harklensian version of the N. T. has a note † appended to it by the translator, Thomas of Harkel, in which he states tha in it he used as its basis the Philoxenian version, correcting it by the aic of Greek MSS. which he had access to in Alexandria. Now on comparing the version now before us with the Harklensian version of the same foui Epistles, it appears beyond doubt that the two versions are not independent of one another. Verse after verse they are substantially identical: the diction of each reflects that of the other: the chief words of one reappear in the other: we find in both not merely the same renderings, but (what is con- clusive) the same misrenderings. So in 2 Peter i. 20, both versions (though varying slightly from one another) fall into the strange mistake of making ἐπιλύσεως a nominative. So again in Jude 6, both are misled by a false etymology to render ἀΐδιοις " unseen." And it is equally certain that of the two it is the Harklensian version that is founded on the version before us, and not *vice versa.* Where they agree substantially, as they mostly do, the Harklensian is simply the other version græcized, according to its

* Moyses of Aghel *ap.* Assem. п. p. 282.   † Adler, p. 47; White, I. p. 561; &c.

habitual manner, by transpositions out of the Syriac into the Greek order;
by insertions—as of the third personal pronouns in lieu of the definite
article which the Syriac lacks; and by the characteristic separation of the
possessive pronoun already noticed, which in the Harklensian is usual,
whereas in the other version it is but occasional and serves for emphasis, or
to represent ἴδιος in the Greek. Where they differ, they usually represent
differing Greek texts: and in such cases the priority of the other version
is attested by the critical apparatus attached to the Harklensian; for the
readings of the former are frequently retained on the Harklensian margin, or stand marked with * in its text. So, *e.g.*, in the passage I have
already dwelt on (2 Peter iii. 10) the Harklensian reads κατακαήσεται,
but on its margin gives εὑρεθήσεται. It thus appears beyond doubt,
on the internal evidence, that the Harklensian is simply a revision of
the other version. But it is equally beyond doubt that the Harklensian
version, on the evidence of its author, had for its basis the Philoxenian
version of Polycarp, and no other. It follows, therefore, by necessary
inference that the version before us, holding as it does to the Harklensian
version the unique relation which the version of Polycarp is known to have
held, is in fact the version of Polycarp; or, as it is usually described, the
original or unrevised Philoxenian. This conclusion is an important one to
bear in mind in the study of the Harklensian version, and of its marginalia
and critical marks. It has been taken for granted by many that Thomas of
Harkel retained the Philoxenian text, and added alternative readings
derived from his Greek authorities on the margin: and there are many
instances confirmatory of that supposition. But the comparison of the two
versions in case of these Epistles yields many instances to the contrary,
where the Philoxenian readings are relegated to the margin, and readings
indicating a different Greek original replace them in the text. It appears
to me probable that Thomas of Harkel formed his text by the exercise of
his critical judgment, in selecting the readings he thought preferable, and
not by mechanical rule; and that the margin accordingly registers neither
(on one hand) the Philoxenian readings only, nor (on the other) new readings from Greek MSS. only; but merely those which he thought less
probable than those he inserted in his text, yet worth recording. A still

more important result of the identification of the version before us as that of Polycarp, and of the comparison of the two versions, is this. We thus learn that in the opening of the sixth century a Syrian scholar, presumably in Mabug, the capital of Euphratensis, had within reach a Greek text closely akin to that of the best uncials now extant; and distinctly superior to that which another Syrian scholar, rather more than a century later, was able to find in Alexandria.*

I pass now to the third and largest part of the *first* or biblical division of our MS.—that which contains the Apocalypse, and consists, as I have stated, of five quires, numbered 1 to 5, though now placed after the quires already described, which are numbered 6 and 7. The first leaf of the first of these five quires is blank. The Apocalypse begins on the recto of the second leaf (being f. 24, if all the blank leaves are included in the numbering). This page is written, not as the former part, in lines of its full width, but in two columns, as are the two following pages, and also f. 52v° and f. 53r°. These lapses into the columnar arrangement probably show that the scribe was accustomed to write on paper of such size as to require to be divided into columns; and in point of fact the pages of the Bodleian O. T., which is from his hand, are so divided. The rest of the book is in lines of full-page width. The first column of the first page (f. 24r°) is headed thus: " In the name of the Father, Son, and Holy Ghost, on the strength of the Holy Trinity, we begin to write the Revelation of John, which is *Abocalebsis* " (ܐܣܘܩܠܒܣܝܣ). Over this stands an ornamental head-piece in black and red, elaborate, but small, being of the width of the column, not of the page. Under it the scribe has written in minute characters (ܐܝܢܐ ܚܛܝܐ ܢܫܟܚ ܪܚܡܐ ܕܨܪ ܘܟܬܒ), "The sinner find mercy who painted and wrote [this]." So in the head-piece of another T. C. D. MS.

* A large fragment of a version of Isaiah, preserved in a Nitrian MS. (*circ.* 600) in the British Museum (Add. 17106), is on independent grounds considered to be probably part of this same original Philoxenian version. Its style agrees well with that of the version above treated of; and on comparing it with the same part of the Isaiah of the Hexaplar version of Paul of Tella (which, as before stated, is a version of the O. T., practically forming one work with the N. T. of Thomas of Harkel), we find exactly the same relations of agreement and variation between their renderings as have been above shown to exist between the two versions of the Four Epistles—an interesting confirmation of the result above arrived at.

from the same hand (B. 5, 19), we read the similar words (ܨܠܝ ܥܠ ܚܛܝܐ ܕܨܪ), "Pray for the sinner who painted [this]" introduced into the intervals of the pattern. The Book is divided into the same twenty-two chapters as in our Bibles, "chapter two" (ܩܦܠܐܘܢ ܒ), and so on, being written in red (in the text), except in case of the first and third chapters: and the address of each of the seven Epistles is written in red likewise (the first partly, the rest entirely). There is no peculiarity to be noted, with one important exception: that of the marginalia which appear in six places. The Book ends on f. 65r°, the third leaf of the fifth of the quires which it occupies; this is numbered 5, and is a half-quire of two sheets only, its last leaf being blank. The subscription is brief: "Ends: and to God [be] glory for ages" (ܫܠܡ ܘܠܐܠܗܐ ܫܘܒܚܐ ܠܥܠܡܝܢ).

I take up first the questions which the peculiar numbering of the quires suggests at first sight. Why did the scribe originally set the Apocalypse first? What is its usual place in the Syriac N. T.? And here we are met by a fact which greatly enhances the value of this part of Ussher's MS.: the extreme rarity of MSS. of the Apocalypse in Syriac. In the last century Ridley (writing in 1761) could only name two; and neither Adler (the best informed Syriac scholar of his day) in 1789, nor J. D. Michaelis in 1788, was able to add to this meagre list. In our own day the Abbé Martin(*Introd. à la Critique du N. T.*, 1883) enters but one of these in his Table of Syriac N. T. MSS., at p. 132, and adds the other at p. 134. None of these scholars was aware of the existence of the MS. now before us. Of the two they knew one was of course the Leyden one, whence De Dieu first printed the text. The other is said to have been in the Library of S. Marco, in Florence, n° 724; and in 1784 Bandini sent Adler a transcript from it of Rev. i. 1, 2. The Leyden copy is still in the library of Leyden University (Cod. Heb. Scal. 18 *). Its colophon gives the scribe's name as "Caspar, from the land of the Indians." The colophon of a liturgical MS. from the hand of the same scribe (in the library of the Orphan House at Halle), describes him as from Malabar, and is dated at Rome, 1580. The Florentine copy is stated by Tregelles (*Introd.* p. 28) to have been written by the Caspar who wrote

---

* *Catal. Codd. Or. Biblioth. Acad. Lugd. Bat.* (1873), mmcccxlv. See Note below, p. 314.

the Leyden MS. If this were so, its text would probably be practically the same as that printed by De Dieu, and therefore of little interest. But Le Long (*Biblioth. S.*, I. p. 191), on the authority of Montfaucon, describes it as written at Rome in 1581, by one Jacob, described as of Hesron (a Maronite therefore, for Hesron is in the Lebanon Patriarchate). It would thus be an independent authority; and there is therefore the more cause to regret that it is no longer forthcoming. Bernstein, writing in 1854 (*De Harkl. N. T. Transl.*, p. 8), informs us that on visiting the library of S. Marco he could find no trace of it. The monk in charge supposed it to have been carried off by the French. It is not, however, recorded in the Bibliothèque Nationale, and must be set down as missing. Its loss, however unfortunate, is in no small measure compensated by the recovery of Ussher's, also (as I have shown) a Maronite copy, only forty-four years later than the missing Florentine one. Its inferiority of age to the Leyden copy is about the same; and on examination I find its text to be distinctly superior. When Ussher, in 1627, wrote of it to Selden (Letter 127), "The Syriac lately set out at Leyden may be much amended by my MS. copy," he was not misled by partiality for his own. And he showed his usual soundness of judgment in fixing on the Apocalypse as the most important item of the contents of our MS. It is the only part which he tells us he himself studied —writing to De Dieu (Letter 154 (on 1st October, 1629, "Ex Apocalypsi tua *quam cum Ms° meo diligenter contuli. . . .*" No notes of his collation, however, are known to exist; nor have we any record of use made of it by De Dieu (so far as I can ascertain), though it was in his hands, as we have seen, for some years. In the Paris Polyglott the Apocalypse in Syriac was printed for the second time, but with so many corrections of text as to satisfy me that its editor must have had a MS. of his own, and that he was thus as independent here of De Dieu as I have already said I believe him to have been of Pococke in the text of the four Epistles. His MS., however, if he had one, is not forthcoming; nor (as I have said, pp. 274, 293) have I found any record of the fate of the MSS. reported to have contained the Apocalypse, which are associated with the names of Moses of Marden, Etzel, and Bellarmine. Thus it appears that the number of available MSS. of the Syriac text of this Book, which was *two* a hundred years ago, after being reduced to one by the loss of the Florence copy, is now raised again to two by the recovery of Ussher's. This result, however, is subject to an important modification. I pass by the collection of extracts from this book in Syriac in the Bodleian (Thurston 13), because it extends only so far as chap. xvii., and is even more recent than Ussher's (1628). But I have to mention that among the Nitrian MSS. of the British Museum there is one (Add. 17127), written A. D. 1088, which contains an elaborate commentary on the Apocalypse, embodying apparently all, or nearly all, the text. I have not learned that anyone has as yet performed the laborious task of putting together the pieces of the text, which would be a matter of much time and patience. I have spent some hours over it, and in the few chapters I have examined here and there I have found it complete, and agreeing substantially with the printed text. If, then, we may assume that this MS. will yield a full text of the Book, we have the total number of available copies raised to three, the last-named copy having the great advantage of being 500 years older than the elder of the other two. But we are no nearer than before to ascertaining how the Syrians placed the Apocalypse in their N. T. For in this Nitrian copy it stands alone, as in that of Leyden, and as (according to Le Long) it stood in that of Florence.* Ussher's is thus the only one in which it is associated with any other N. T. book. In the description (above, p. 274, n.) of the contents of the MS. sent to Bellarmine by Paul V., the Apocalypse is named before the Four Epistles. This is perhaps accidental, but it may possibly imply that such was the order in that MS. And thus the volume out of which the scribe employed by Davies copied the " N. T. parcels " of Ussher's MS. (if, indeed, we are to suppose them to have been derived from any one such volume), may have presented them in the like order; the Apocalypse following first after the books recognized by the Peshitto canon, and then the disputed Pericope and the four Epistles classed as Antilegomena, subjoined as an appendix. But it seems more likely that the priority given to the Apocalypse was casual, or determined by its greater length only ; and that the exemplar whence the scribe copied it was a several volume, separate from that whence he derived the four

---

* The Abbé Martin (l. l.) regards this Florence MS. as a complete N. T. ; but this seems to be a misapprehension.

Epistles; possibly, like the Leyden copy, containing the Apocalypse alone. The Apocalypse, as it stands in Ussher's MS., contains three more or less distinct series of evidences that the original which it reproduces was of different character from the original of the Four Epistles which are bound up with it. The first is the *punctuation :* but on this I do not lay stress. For though it is observable, as I have said, that the lozenges, which in the Apocalypse mark all the larger divisions, occur but twice in the four Epistles; yet this may be accounted for by the shortness of the Epistles, rendering such divisions less necessary. But the second is more significant—the *capitulation.* The division of the Apocalypse into the usual Western twenty-two chapters, while 2 Peter is divided only once, at the 9th verse of chap. ii., where a Syrian lesson began, leads us to conclude that the immediate exemplar of the Apocalypse of our MS. was one which had, while that of the Four Epistles was one which had not, come under Western influences. The third is the *marginal notation.* No notes are found on the margin of the Epistles; six stand on that of the Apocalypse; all within the first 34 of its 83 pages—a fact which suggests that the exemplar would have supplied more had the scribe's industry not abated as he went on. At least it had some marginal notes; and therefore was presumably detached from, and unlike, the exemplar of the Epistles, which (in this MS., and usually) are not furnished with any marginalia.

But a more interesting question than this of the immediate derivation of the text lies behind—that, namely, of the authorship of the version. When the existence of the Apocalypse in Syriac was first made known, the suspicion was thrown out that the version was a recent one, made by Maronite scholars. De Dieu (*Præf. in Apoc.*) sufficiently refutes this surmise, by pointing out that the Greek text underlying the version as he published it often widely differs from that printed under Papal authority, or that implied by the Vulgate, such as the Maronites, being entirely under Romish control, would certainly have followed. But since the Nitrian MS. (Add. 17127) above described has come to light the antiquity of the version is vindicated, inasmuch as it is thus directly demonstrated to have been in currency over 800 years ago. However, no Syrian authority on the subject of the version of the Bible has named the translator of the Apocalypse;

and we have only the negative fact, admitted by all, that this Book was not in the Peshitto, while we are not informed whether either of the later versions contained it. Yet when we read that Polycarp in 508, and Thomas in 616, translated the N. T., we may fairly presume that the statement includes the Apocalypse—especially as in case of Thomas we know, and in case of Polycarp have seen good reason to believe, that it does include the Four Epistles which are associated with the Apocalypse as being omitted from the Peshitto. One external testimony only has been adduced in the matter : it is that of Jacob of Hesron, the scribe of the Florence MS., who, as it is stated, cited in his colophon a subscription from his exemplar, professing to be written by Thomas of Harkel and to claim the version as his. Against this is to be set the negative evidence of the recently acquired Cambridge MS. (Add. 1700), which contains the N. T. in the Harklensian version, omitting only the Apocalypse. Unfortunately, the only other MS. of the Harklensian N. T. which seems ever to have been complete (another of Ridley's, in New Coll. Library, No. 333) is mutilated at the end, so that it is uncertain whether the Apocalypse ever formed part of it. But though we are thus unable to verify the statement of the scribe, it must be admitted that the internal evidence of the Syriac text gives it much probability. After the Harklensian manner, it græcizes : it forces words out of the Syriac into the Greek order, uses the third personal pronoun to represent the Greek article, separates the possessive pronoun as in Greek, and often adopts Greek words, merely transliterating them into Syriac (as θρόνος, φιάλη, ἄψινθος, and the names of the precious stones throughout, &c.). I incline therefore to the opinion, advanced in the last century by Ridley and by Storr, and recently adopted by Davidson, that this Syriac Apocalypse belongs to the Harklensian N. T. Adler, followed by Marsh, and of late by Tregelles, has controverted this view (p. 78). His arguments are far from convincing, and in brief come to this, that some of the peculiarities of Thomas's method of rendering do not appear in this book so uniformly as in the books known to be rendered by him. We may grant all this, and yet refuse to admit it as conclusive against the opinion that the version was made by Thomas; for he may well be supposed to have relaxed somewhat of the rigidity of his very artificial manner as he drew near the close of his long work. But in some points Adler has over-stated his case against the Harklensian authorship of the version. One Harklensian characteristic which he instances as infrequent in the Syriac Apocalypse, the adoption of Greek words, is, as I have shown, largely found in it; another, the writing of proper names in the Greek form, is a matter in which the usage of transcribers even of acknowledged Harklensian texts is found to vary. Of deviation in this Book from the close reproduction of the Greek which Thomas affected, he adduces but two definite examples; and these both break down when examined. The translator, he says, (a) omits the explanatory words, ἀρχὴ καὶ τέλος, which follow τὸ A καὶ τὸ Ω, in i. 8; whereas Thomas never fails to translate such words : and (b) in i. 9 he neglects to represent the συν- of συγκοινωνός; while in the other N. T. places where the word occurs (but three in all) Thomas resolves it into two words, so as to express the compound. But (a) the Greek text which the translator had before him probably omitted ἀρχὴ καὶ τέλος from the former verse, as our Revised Version does, with the majority of the best authorities : and (b) in the latter verse it may well have read the simple κοινωνός, as many (though not most) Greek cursives do. Probably the Florence MS., if it could be recovered, would yield information bearing on this question of the Harklensian authorship of our version; if one may judge by the two verses (i. 1 and 2) which are all we now have of it, already mentioned as printed by Adler from Bandini's transcript. They contain a token of Harklensian workmanship which Adler failed to perceive. In the Harklensian text, as is well known, asterisks are attached to certain words, usually to denote insertions into the text, sometimes to refer to Greek words written in the margin. Now, in the second verse as given in the Florence text, in the words ὅσα εἶδεν, the ὅσα is resolved into two words (ܐܠܝܢ ܠܟܠ), and to the second word (ܐܠܝܢ), which is pleonastic, an asterisk is attached, which does not appear in the Leyden text, nor in Ussher's. But it is noteworthy that, whereas the asteriscised word is omitted from the Leyden text, I find it inserted in Ussher's. Thomas of Harkel's rendering of this word ὅσος varies; but when I point out that a similar pleonastic rendering of ὅσα is found in the Harklensian version of the ὅσα ἐστὶν ἀληθῆ of Philipp. iv. 8, with an asterisk similarly attached to refer to the Greek ὅσα which is written in the margin, it will be seen that the asterisk of the Florence MS. at i. 2 probably indicates that ὅσα was on its margin or that of its exemplar, but dropped out in transcription. And thus this asterisk, trivial as it may seem, becomes a significant piece of evidence. (See farther, below, p. 314).

I now proceed to the testimony of Ussher's MS. on this question, which I can show to be ampler and more distinct on the same side. It is derived from the marginal notes, six in number, which I have mentioned as peculiar to this part of the MS. Among the earliest are two notes on the names of Ephesus and Smyrna, the first two Churches addressed. In the first, Ephesus is styled "the assembly of the Apostles" (ܒܝܫܝܟ ܐܠܝܫܠܝܟ ܩܗܘܗ‍ܐ ܟܗ). In the second, Smyrna is explained "bitterness," and is styled "the heap of the witness" (or, "the tomb of the martyr," ܣܐܩܣܠܝ ܗܝ ܣܘܪܝܠܝ ܟܗ‍ܝ ܩܣܢ‍ܝ ܟ‍ܝ). The presumption is, that in the exemplar whence these notes were derived, like notes were attached to the names of the remaining five Churches. Notes of the same nature are found on the Harklensian margin. So at Acts xii. 13 the name of Rhoda is explained ܗܝ ܪܗܘܕܠܝ. And at Acts x. 1 the name of Cornelius has an interpretation appended which I do not quote for its philological value, ܗܝ ܟܘܣ‍ܝ ܣܡܣܟ‍ܝ, *i. e.*, "the pupil of the sun," as if κόρην + ἥλιος! Again, the note at 1 Pet. iii. 3, where χρυσία is explained "various jewels" (ܗܝ‍ܩ ܟܣܣ‍ܝ ܣܡܣܒܩܐ‍ܝ ܟܗ), and that at 2 Pet. i. 13, interpreting σκήνωμα to mean "body" (ܟܘܣܟ‍ܝ ܟܣܟ‍ܝ ܟܗ‍ܝ), are precisely analogous to those on the churches named Rev. ii. 1, 8. Of the rest of the marginalia I pass over two as possibly mere scribe's corrections; but the two which remain are noticeable as indicating the translator's knowledge of various readings of the Greek. One is at ii. 25, where for the ܟ‍ܝ ("I *come*") of the text, he offers on his margin the alternative ܐܠܩ‍ܣ ("I *open*"), showing that he was aware of the reading ἀνοίξω (for ἂν ἥξω), which is found in one uncial (B) and many cursive Greek texts. The remaining one is at ix. 19, where the Received Text reads ἐν τῷ στόματι αὐτῶν only, omitting καὶ ἐν ταῖς οὐραῖς αὐτῶν, which the best MSS. add. The Syriac as given in the Leyden MS. renders these words. Ussher's omits them, but inserts them in the margin; thus apparently preserving evidence that the translator had both readings before him.

The result then is, that the margin of our MS. adds appreciably to the evidence, already considerable, in favour of the opinion that this translation of the Apocalypse into Syriac was made by Thomas of Harkel. If it was his (I may here observe), the question of the place of the Apocalypse in the Syriac N. T. is settled so far as his authority can settle it. For in the New Coll. MS. (333), for the Apocalypse no place is left but the last, and it can hardly have stood anywhere in the archetype of the Cambridge MS. (Add. 1700) but at the end; else that MS. would not have left it out. One argument has been advanced against his authorship to which little weight is due—that, namely, which rests on the alleged inferiority of the translation of this book in comparison with the recognized work of Thomas. For generally no translator is always equal to himself, and in the course of a long work, especially towards the end, weariness will admit errors. And in particular such errors are naturally to be expected in the version (by whatever translator made) of a book in which the guidance of the Peshitto was wanting. How capable Thomas was of blundering under such circumstances appears from the two instances I have already adduced from the Four Epistles (2 Pet. i. 20; Jude 6), where, in the absence of the Peshitto, he has allowed himself to be misled into following Polycarp's mistakes; though, in case of the word ἀΐδιος, he had translated it correctly in the only other place where it occurs in the N. T., Rom. i. 20. The fact is, I suspect, that this version has been unduly discredited by one mistranslation which disfigures it, so signal that every writer on the subject mentions it, and so ludicrous that no one who has ever heard of it can forget it. In viii. 13, the words ἀετοῦ πετομένου ἐν μεσουρανήματι are rendered "an eagle flying in the midst which had a tail of blood"! (ܟܘܦ ܫܡܢܐ ܢܐܪܐ ܕܕܡܐ ܢܛܝܪܐ ܕܠܗ ܕܒܠܬ). This blunder, amazing as it seems, is easily explained. The word μεσουράνημα, not previously found in the N. T. (though it occurs in two subsequent places of the Apocalypse), was strange to the translator, and it resolved itself in his eyes into three, μέσῳ, οὐράν, ἥματι (which last he read as αἵματι). The rest he supplied, with the unhappy result as it stands.* In xiv. 6, where the word is next met with, in the sentence ἀγγε-

* As if to show that a deeper depth of absurdity was not unattainable, De Dieu has

λον πετόμενον ἐν μεσουρανήματι, ἔχοντα εὐαγγέλιον αἰώνιον, it seems to have struck the translator that the tail, which in the former passage he naturally assigned to the eagle, would not suit the angel: and accordingly he drops it, reads οὐραν as οὐρανῷ, but retains αἵματι, rendering, "an angel flying in heaven, having *in blood* the everlasting Gospel." It is extraordinary that at xix. 17, where the word appears for the last time, he renders τοῖς ὀρνέοις τοῖς πετομένοις ἐν μεσουρανήματι quite correctly. To have made so huge a blunder, then by degrees to have found it out, and yet not to have turned back and corrected it, undoubtedly shows a strong case against our trans-lator of ignorance at first and carelessness afterwards. But it is worth while to point out how this extreme instance illustrates the quantity of informa-tion derivable from a translation that strives to be faithful, even though it bears here and there marks of ignorance or carelessness. (1°) As to the *nationality* of the translator. I infer that Thomas was a Syrian trying to translate Greek, and not a Greek trying to write Syriac; for the utter unconsciousness of case-endings apparent in this blunder bespeaks a writer born to the use of a Semitic tongue to which case-endings were unknown. The misrendering of ἐπιλύσεως (2 Pet. i. 20) gives ground for a like infe-rence, extending to Polycarp. (2°) As to his *identification*. I consider that this misrendering, so far from being an argument against ascribing this version to Thomas, goes the other way. The instances I have given show what enormities in the shape of Greek Thomas was capable of; and I submit that the man who made αἵματι out of the last three syllables of μεσουρανήματι may well be the same as he who read ἥλιος in the last three syllables of Κορνήλιος—to say nothing of the analogy between the pendent accusatives, οὐρὰν in the one case, and κόρην in the other. (3°) As to the *Greek text*. I remark that if he had rendered μεσουρανήματι correctly in viii. 13, we should have missed two facts which we gather from his mistakes. For, *first*, by finding "a tail" in the middle of the word, he shows that he was unaware of the reading ἄγγελος (for ἀετός), which is that of the Authorized (though not of the Revised) Version, after the Received

mistranslated this mistranslation, thus, "*In medio cauda quæ sanguinem habet.*" The Paris Polyglott, followed by Walton, corrects this.

Text and many cursives. And, *secondly*, by reading the end of the word as αἵματι, he testifies that his Greek MS. wrote μεσουρανήματι, and not in the alternative form, μεσουρανίσματι. (4°) In another way, I have found this same blunder of use in giving a ready answer to a question which might else have been hard to solve. In examining the MS. Syriac Commentary on the Apocalypse which I have mentioned, I became curious to ascertain whether it was the work of a Syrian divine, or a translation from a Greek one; when it occurred to me that the note on viii. 13 would serve as a test. I found it to run as follows:—"*An eagle which flew in heaven, which had a tail of blood.* Here he teaches, in saying that he had a tail of blood, that the God who spake with Moses, and went before the sons of Israel by night in a pillar of fire, and by day in a cloud—even he, though he was God, in the latter times came as flesh, and was killed and died for our salvation. Because of this John saith that he had a tail of blood." My question was answered. It was clear that the author of this comment knew the Apocalypse only in Syriac.

But I do not by any means imply that the value of this version lies merely or mainly in the facts which may thus be indirectly inferred from its aberrations. Its mistakes are far from numerous, and the one I have instanced is anything but a fair sample of the entire work. On the whole, it renders its sublime original correctly and with dignity: indeed there are parts of it where the revelations made to the Apocalyptist seem to find happier utterance in the Syriac than in the Greek in which he wrote them down. Every reader of the opening salutation must have felt how the Greek language labours and breaks down under the strain put upon it when charged with the enunciation of His eternal Being from whom the greeting comes, ἀπὸ ὁ ὢν καὶ ὁ ἦν καὶ ὁ ἐρχόμενος. In the Syriac (as in our English) the happy lack of inflexions clears away the solecisms that mar the Greek phrase, and the thought, as St. John conceived it, discloses itself in worthier expression when read back into the congenial diction of an idiom closely akin to the native speech in which it first shaped itself into words within his spirit—ܐܝܢܐ܂ ܗܘ ܗܘܐ ܘܐܝܬܘܗܝ܂ ܗܘ ܘܐܝܬܘܗܝ܂ ܗܘ ܡܢ.

The importance of this version for critical purposes is not slight. In several passages it yields such decisive evidence of the readings of the MS.

which was its original, as to be a considerable accession to the authorities, not very abundant, for the Greek text of this part of the N. T. Accordingly it has been largely used by Tischendorf and others who have laboured in the field of textual criticism : and in order to bring out its evidence in a more correct and distinct shape, I believe it will be well worth while to make that complete comparison of our MS. with De Dieu's text which Ussher indicated 250 years ago as a work that ought to be done. The British Museum copy also awaits, and (considering its much higher date) is still more likely to repay, thorough collation. Possibly the Florence MS. may some day be recovered, and other missing copies may turn up, or copies hitherto unrecorded may be acquired in the East. Thus an approximately perfect text of the version may ultimately be restored, and the question of its authorship finally settled. Meantime, as a first step towards these results, I have made some progress in a collation of this MS.

In all that I have thus far written, I have assumed that this Syriac Apocalypse is not part of the same version as that to which the Four Epistles associated with it in our MS. belong ; for on that head the internal evidence is conclusive. Its method is quite distinct from theirs, and is unquestionably Harklensian ; insomuch that the critics who refuse to admit it to be the work of Thomas ascribe it to a translator who tried to imitate his manner. The question however remains—Did the translator (whether Thomas or another) translate directly from the Greek, or did he work, as Thomas is known to have done in all his recognized translations, on the lines of a version made a century before by Polycarp for Philoxenus ? I find only two pieces of evidence adducible towards solving this question. The first is a copy in Syriac of the passage Rev. vii. 1–8, contained in another Nitrian MS. in the British Museum (Add. 17193, f. 146), of A.D. 874, resembling, but not identical with, the rendering of the same passage given in the version as printed ; which latter varies from it in much the same manner and degree as the Harklensian text of the Four Epistles varies from that which I have discussed above. The second is a like extract from Rev. xvii. (3–6), found in a Syriac catena on Genesis which is printed among the works of Ephraim Syrus (Roman ed., tom. i. (Syr.), pp. 116 ff. : see p. 102), but is known to consist in part of selections from the writings of Jacob of

Edessa (*circ.* 700). In this passage the variations from the printed version are on the whole similar in kind to those that are found in the former one; but they are more considerable in amount, and include (within four verses) evidence of two various readings of the Greek. Both passages thus lend themselves very well to the hypothesis that they may be fragments of a lost version by Polycarp, used as a basis by the author of the existing version. But, as regards the second passage, it may well have been rendered by Jacob of Edessa himself, who is known to have been a translator of Scripture (though we are not informed that he translated any part of the *New* Testament). And we have no proof, as regards either passage, that it ever formed part of a complete translation of the Book to which it belongs. Both may have been translated merely as detached extracts; and it would be unsafe to build on either, or both, an hypothesis of a version by Polycarp, or anyone else, preceding and underlying the version before us. If conclusive proof of the existence of such a version should hereafter come to light, it will in some measure modify the evidential results obtainable from the existing version. So long as we accept this version as the work of Thomas, or an assistant or disciple of his, we must estimate it for purposes of Greek textual criticism as simply equivalent to a Greek MS. which was in repute in Alexandria at the beginning of the seventh century. But if we discover that he based it on a previous version, its proper and direct evidence becomes mixed with that which it repeats at second-hand from another MS. of a different place and of an earlier date.

I have now completed my account of the *first* or biblical division of the MS., and have left myself room for but a brief survey of the *second*, of which indeed I have as yet been able to make but a superficial examination. It is separated from the former division by a blank half-quire, similar to that which separates the Apocalypse from the Epistles, and it is made up of four quires, numbered 1 to 4, the last being of four sheets only, the others of five. Of the thirty-eight leaves it thus contains, the first only is blank; the rest are occupied with the Tractate of Ephraim, which is the whole of its contents. At the top of the second leaf of the first quire stands a head-piece in black and red, resembling in design that which is at the beginning of the *Pericope de Adultera*. Then comes the heading, "In the name of God that liveth for ever, we begin to write a little from the tractates of our father, honoured and blessed, Mar Ephraim, concerning the Love of Wisdom and Knowledge (ܠܐ ܕܚܡܬܐ ܘܡܕܥܐ). And there are twenty-two sayings. The first, in which is the letter Olaph." Then follows accordingly the first of these "sayings," or sections, beginning with ܐ; and then the rest in order, twenty-two in all, after the number of the Semitic alphabet, each beginning with its letter (as in Ps. cxix.). Each, moreover, consists of twenty-two verses, having a like alphabetical arrangement (as in Lamentations), the first beginning from ܐ and ending with ܬ, the second from ܒ and ending with ܐ, and so on; till the last, beginning with ܬ, ends with ܫ. The colophon is simply "Ends; and to Jah [be] δόξα. Year 1626." (ܫܠܡ ܘܠܗ ܬܫܒܘܚܬܐ ܫܢܬ ܐܠܦ.)

Similar alphabetical compositions are frequent among the writings of Ephraim; but I have not met with any other arranged exactly after the elaborate fashion of this. This copy of it is, so far as I know, unique; and I find no trace of it in the great Roman edition of Ephraim, or in any collection of his works, Syriac or translated, to which I have had access. A much shorter Tractate, also alphabetical, with a similar title, *On the Love of Learning* (ܠܐ ܕܚܡܬ ܝܘܠܦܢܐ), is well known; it was by order of Pope Gregory XIII. printed for distribution among the Maronite youth. A Latin version of it is included in Gerard Voss's Latin edition of Ephraim (1603), p. 267; and the Syriac text is given in the Roman edition (tom. ii. (Syr.) p. 336), where it is printed among the *Sermones Exegetici*, with the text Prov. v. 1. A copy of it is among the *Homilies* of Ephraim in another T.C.D. MS. (B. 5. 19), which I have mentioned above (p. 280) as described by Ussher in a letter (188) to De Dieu in 1633, and as bearing his autograph signature. But this composition contains but forty-four verses, two for each letter, and is thus much shorter than the Tractate in the MS. now before us, from which it is quite distinct. Ussher had read it; for in this letter he notices that it is one of those included in Voss's version, and adds that Isaac Sciadrensis had printed it in Syriac at Rome in 1618, but had failed to observe its alphabetic structure; having displaced the first word so as to make the first verse begin with ܗܘ instead of ܐܠܗܐ. The first line is (ܐܠܗܐ ܗܘ ܝܘܠܦܢܐ ܗܒ ܠܗ ܕܝܘܠܦܢܐ), " O God, bestow learning on him

.that loves learning." It is thus of the nature of a prayer or hymn. The Tractate in the present MS. is rather a hortatory treatise, following the manner and often adopting the words of the Book of Proverbs ; which Ephraim imitated also in his tractates Κατὰ μίμησιν τῶν Παροιμίων, extant in Greek, and printed in the Roman edition, tom. I. (Gr.), p. 70. Its opening is:—

"I. 1. O thou that desirest to be made wise, pray that thou mayst hear ; and in thy understanding fix my sayings with my interpretations.

"2. With all thy possessions and with all thy goods, buy my instructions; which are very sweet, and make thee wise and make thee glad."

It closes as follows (cp. Prov. xv. 1 ; x. 10):—

"XXII. 21. The words of the mouth turn away anger, if they are soft: but if they are grievous, they stir up clamour with contention.

"22. He maketh peace who reproveth his neighbour openly : and he that winketh, causeth sorrow."

NOTE ADDED IN THE PRESS.*

Since the above Paper was read, I have seen two of the MSS. above referred to : the Amsterdam N. T. (No. 184), and the Leyden Apocalypse. I subjoin a brief note of the results of my inspection.

I desire to express my thanks to Dr. H. C. Rogge, Librarian of the Amsterdam Seminary of Remonstrants, for his kindness in permitting me to collate the text of the Four Minor Catholic Epistles from the former MS.; and to Dr. M. Th. Houtsma, Adj. Interpres Legati Warneriani, of the University of Leyden, who gave me every facility for examining the latter.

I. Wetstein's MS. (Amsterdam No. 184) contains the Acts, with Epistles as specified above, p. 274, n., written on seventeen quires (each of five sheets), numbered from 18 to 34 inclusive. The first has lost its first three leaves, and the last its concluding leaf, so that 166 leaves remain. Thus the first 17 quires and 3 leaves of the 18th, of the book as originally made up in 34 quires, are wanting. On the recto of leaf 1, being 4th of the quire numbered

* In the foregoing pages I have not mentioned the Cambridge MS., Oo. 1, 2, which contains the Apocalypse, but is described as modern.

18 (now 1st quire), the Book of Acts begins, with its heading duly prefixed.
The volume has therefore been intentionally divided at this place, and the
173 leaves which have been removed no doubt contained the Gospels. For
them about 130 leaves would suffice, so that there would be some 40 leaves
over. These may have been occupied by preliminary matter; but may
possibly (though not probably) have also contained the Apocalypse, which
would fill about 20 leaves. The Four Minor Catholic Epistles in this MS.
are of the ante-Harklensian version (which no doubt is what Beelen means
when he describes it as "Philoxenian,"—Prolegg., p. x.). The text, though
inferior to the older Nitrian and probably contemporary Williams MSS., is
superior to the Maronite text of the Oxford and Dublin copies. It omits the
interpolated negative from 2 Pet. iii. 10; but exhibits the faulty reading
of ii. 1 (see above, p. 295). In four places it gives, *prima manu*, alternative
readings on the margin, all from the Harklensian version (viz. 2 Pet. iii. 5,
10; 2 John 8; 3 John 7). The scribe must therefore have had a Harklensian
copy at hand; and this probably accounts for the Harklensian rendering
(countenanced by no Greek MS.) which has crept into the text, Jude 7.

II. Scaliger's MS. (Cod. Scalig. 18 (Syr.) Leyden) is written in a Maronite hand. The scribe divides the text throughout by the usual lozenge and
other like marks, but does not note the chapters or verses as given by
De Dieu. The chapters have been marked on the margin by a later hand,
which has also supplied sundry corrections. One important feature of this
MS. De Dieu has omitted to reproduce—the insertion of asterisks. Of these,
37 or 38 occur in the text, all *prima manu:* most of them probably—several
certainly—relating to various readings or renderings of the Greek. Thus
the closer examination of this MS. adds manifold confirmation to the argument for assigning this version to Thomas, which I have above (p. 305) drawn
from the single asterisk recorded from the Florence MS. The following is
a select list of words whose Syriac equivalents are in this MS. marked *.
Apoc. ii. 9 (also 13) τὰ ἔργα; iii. 3, ἐπί σε; v. 7, τὸ βιβλίον; xi. 1, καὶ ὁ ἄγγελος εἰστήκει; xi. 5, οὕτως; xi. 16, τοῦ θρόνου; xiii. 10, συνάγει; xiii. 17,
τοῦ ὀνόματος; xiv. 5, γάρ; xiv. 18, ἐξῆλθεν; xv. 6, οἱ ἦσαν; xix. 1, καὶ ἡ
τίμη; xix. 12, ὀνόματα γεγραμμένα καί; xix. 15, δίστομος; xxi. 3, Θεὸς αὐτῶν;
xxi. 8, καὶ ἁμαρτωλοῖς; xxii. 14, οἱ ποιοῦντες τὰς ἐντολὰς αὐτοῦ.

THE

TRANSACTIONS

OF THE

ROYAL IRISH ACADEMY

VOLUME XXVII.

POLITE LITERATURE AND ANTIQUITIES.

DUBLIN:

PUBLISHED BY THE ACADEMY,

AT THEIR HOUSE, 19, DAWSON-STREET.

1877–1886.

DUBLIN:

PRINTED AT THE UNIVERSITY PRESS, BY PONSONBY & WELDRICK, PRINTERS TO THE ROYAL IRISH ACADEMY;
AND SOLD AT THE ACADEMY HOUSE; ALSO BY HODGES, FIGGIS, & CO., 104, GRAFTON-STREET, DUBLIN;
AND WILLIAMS & NORGATE, 14, HENRIETTA-STREET, COVENT GARDEN, LONDON.

CONTENTS.

** The date of reading will be found prefixed to each Paper. The date of publication, as inserted in the above Table of Contents of this Volume, is that when the Paper was laid in a printed form on the Table of the Academy; or, when the Academy was not in Session, the date when it was forwarded to the Academy's Booksellers.

THE ACADEMY *desire it to be understood, that they are not answerable for any opinion, representation of facts, or train of reasoning, that may appear in the following Papers. The Authors of the several Essays are alone responsible for their contents.*

TRANSACTIONS, VOL. XXVIII. (SCIENCE).

www.ingramcontent.com/pod-product-compliance
Lightning Source LLC
Chambersburg PA
CBHW021232260626
47172CB00002B/728